Also by Dani Ryan

THE RYDER BROTHERS

A series of interconnected standalone contemporary romances

Forever My Protector

Forever My Ranger

Forever My Soldier

Forever My Guardian

THE HURRICANES

A series of interconnected standalone rom-coms

It Just Happened

THE MORELLI SISTERS

A series of interconnected standalone rom-coms

Don't Tell Me Twice

Say It Isn't So

UP TO SNOW GOOD

DANI RYAN

Printed and bound in the United States of America, POD.
ISBN 979-8330397976 (paperback)

Author's Note

Thank you for picking up this first book and joining me in Silver Springs for this interconnected standalone rom-com series! It's meant to be a fun, quick festive read that you can enjoy in between baking cookies and decking the halls to your favorite holiday songs.

I hope you enjoy this grumpy x sunshine rom-com as much as I've enjoyed writing it!

Warm wishes this holiday season!

With much love,
Dani

P.S. Sign up for my newsletter and stay up-to-date on all my latest, including new releases and promotions. Plus, be among the first to know about exciting news. Did I forget to mention you'll also get a bonus scene from one of my books when you subscribe?

To my grandmother, book lover, Belle and Beast lover,

and most importantly my biggest cheerleader.

You always wanted me to write.

I hope you're smiling down on this one.

Prologue

Once upon a time there was a young boy who lived in a penthouse that overlooked Central Park. While it may have seemed to an outsider's eye that he had everything he could ever want, he was missing the one thing a young boy needed—his parent's love.

Then something incredible happened, something truly extraordinary—he caught the eye of a beautiful girl who said she thought him to be handsome and smart. Only later was it revealed that she was using him to make another jealous. When the charade was up, she shunned him, unbelieving that he could ever think a girl like her could like a boy like him.

Years later, the girl, a woman now, saw him again and tried to apologize, but it was too late, for he had grown up to become guarded and grumpy.

Ashamed and believing that he was not worthy of love, he concealed himself and spent his days in his office, at his penthouse, or on a work trip that always seemed to last far too long for his liking.

As the years passed, he continued to lose hope in love and happiness. For who could ever learn to love a man like him?

Chapter One

Bo

THE PAST

"Hey, I'm Izzy."

Did you hear that? It was the sound of this woman's voice.

It was pleasing to the ear, but also sweet, so sweet in fact I feared I'd get a cavity just listening to it.

It was mellifluous, but not angels singing or anything, a notch just below that.

"It's really nice meeting you," she said and went on. And on. And on.

I wouldn't bore you with the play by play, but what I would say was that I thought we reached a point where I wanted to clench my jaw so tight that I might've cracked a molar. *Man, I needed a drink.*

She smiled at me, so wide in fact that I wondered if her face was tired. What I wanted to say was, "No need to hurt your face on my account." But something told me she smiled like that often. So instead I said, "It's great meeting you, too. I'm Bo."

She placed both hands behind her head, fussing with her hair. Then she dropped her hands. "So you want a drink?" she asked me, practically shouting now as the bar grew louder.

I nodded. Definitely. Absolutely. One-million percent. "Sure."

I heard the sound of a bell being rung and turned to see a big, burly man standing on a table, shouting something I didn't quite catch. "What's that about?"

"That's Hank. He's telling everyone it's karaoke time. Kicks off when the bell rings, but for newcomers he stands on a table and formally announces it," she paused and pointed, "just like that to alert them to what's going on." Then she giggled. "Well, tries to anyway. It can get pretty rowdy in here on a Friday night as you can tell."

After ordering our drinks, I turned in my seat and looked out at the dance floor, tilting my head. "Looks like Fiona and Louie had no trouble ditching us."

She looked, too, and then turned back around, waving a hand in the air. "Eh, they're in love."

"Love," I repeated the word, but then swore not to say it again for fear that, like with the boogeyman, something would happen if I said it too many times.

The whole notion of love was ridiculous and basically far-fetched. I'd been "in love" before, but it was a conscious choice. And there laid the ridiculousness of love. There was no such thing as falling in love or tripping or stumbling or whatever you wanted to call it. Why couldn't people see love for it really was? I would have more respect for the whole notion if people just said it like it was: *I have decided to be in love with this person so that we can tie ourselves together with a piece of paper in a supposedly sacred union. Then we can have babies and brag about the family tree we've created all because we decided to love each other.*

That was what Louie and Fiona were celebrating, in my opinion. Their conscious decision to love one another. Their daily commitment to each other. That was what their wedding was all about.

What? Just because I was the best man didn't mean I needed to have stars in my eyes for the whole concept.

And because you were probably already thinking it— yes, I believed Valentine's Day was concocted by chocolate and greeting card companies who got together to make money. Frankly, it was genius. And the chocolate and card companies weren't the only ones to make out like bandits on that day, but we were going way off topic there.

Izzy ran a hand across the rim of her glass. "Something tells me you're not the romantic type."

No argument there. I took a sip of my scotch and shrugged. "What, like buy a girl flowers and bring her boxes of chocolates?"

She quirked a brow and placed a hand on my arm. Her hand was small and her touch delicate. Honestly, as I looked down at it, I actually imagined holding it in my own.

No way! I shook my head and pushed those thoughts away. Far, far away. Thoughts like those were going to get me nowhere.

It was this whole wedding bull. What was it about weddings that made people feel extra lonely, like it held a magnifying glass to the one part of your life you cared to not highlight so much? You know, the one where you came home every night to an empty house?

A woman like Izzy shouldn't be anywhere near a man like me. She was way too happy and optimistic. I, on the other hand, prided myself on being a realist. Hence the reason I could see love for what it really was—malarkey.

Clearing her throat, she pulled her hand back and smiled, the smile reaching the corners of her eyes. "Sure, flowers and chocolate are nice, but love is more than thinking about someone. It's like," she stopped, clearly searching for the words. Then she placed a hand on her chest and gasped. "Like that."

I gave her a puzzled expression and cocked a brow. "Like gasping?"

"No." She chuckled. "Like getting the wind knocked out of you."

"Sounds uncomfortable."

She pursed her lips. "It's hard to explain."

I held my glass in my hands. "Maybe so, but I guess I see what you're saying."

"So?" she prompted and looked at me expectantly.

I shook my head. "So, what?" *What was she waiting for?*

"Have you ever been in love before?"

Sighing, I sat back and released the grip I had on my glass. "Yes, but something tells me our past relationship experiences are drastically different," I explained, not wanting to go back to that place, but I could tell I needed to explain otherwise this might never end. "She wasn't who I thought she was."

A pout on her lips, she leaned forward and placed her hand on my arm again. "I'm sorry, Bo."

Thankfully, Fiona walked up just then and announced, "Come on, it's karaoke time."

Not that I had any clue what she wanted us to do about it and where we were going. I looked at Louie and shook my head. As my best friend he should already know I wasn't getting up on stage and singing no matter how many drinks they plied me with.

Izzy, much to my surprise, seemed to feel the same way. Shaking her head, she insisted, "Uh-uh! No way."

"Izzy," Fiona said, tugging on her arm. "Come on."

"Fine, but I need at least two tequila shots before getting up there," Izzy conceded. "How about you, Bo?"

I looked at Louie again who was only laughing, sipping his beer. "What'd you expect, buddy? It's karaoke night."

I shook my head. "Sorry. I'll watch."

"Told you he wouldn't play ball," Louie said to Fiona as he wrapped his arm around her waist and brought her close.

She turned to me and now I felt the stare of six eyes on me, but I wasn't budging on this one. There were three things I would never do. Okay, well, there were a lot of things, but these three were non-negotiable.

First, skinny dipping. An ex-girlfriend told me it was romantic and fun, but we could just as easily get naked and hop in the shower together. See, no clothes and water. Same thing.

Second, karaoke.

And, third, let someone get close enough to break my heart. Been there, done that.

Before you went feeling sorry for me, I didn't need sympathy. I needed to be smart enough to know that I wasn't the guy that got the girl.

Izzy threw back her drink before slamming the glass back down. "All right!" she announced and stood. "Let's do this. Senior year pop meets rock?" she asked her friend.

"You know it!"

"And, Bo, I haven't forgotten about you," Izzy said before walking away with Fiona, their arms intertwined. "You need fun in your life. And I accept the challenge."

I looked from her to Louie, who only tossed his hands up in the air. "No idea, man," he said when they were out of earshot.

I didn't understand it, there were millions of women he could've picked from. Literally anyone else.

And it wasn't Fiona. She was great.

It was Izzy.

"You couldn't get engaged to literally any other woman than that one's best friend?"

Louie laughed and sat back, his eyes on the stage. "Stop. She's not that bad," he replied.

I sighed, my eyes on her, watching as she laughed and smiled. "She's just so—"

"Cheerful?" Louie supplied. "Yeah, I know. I figured it might just kill you."

Looking at the bottom of my glass as the liquid hit my lips, I tried, "Maybe it won't be so bad at the wedding. She'll be busy with Fiona for most of it, right?"

And the fact that she was the maid of honor and I was the best man and we'd be spending a decent amount of time together did not elude me.

Chapter Two

From: izzydoesbooks@mymail.com
To: bo@grantandco.com
Subject: Fiona and Louie

Bo, hi! We met at karaoke night a few months back with Fiona and Louie. Anyway, since you're Louie's best man and I'm Fi's maid of honor, I figured I'd reach out. You probably already know this, but they're going for a Christmas Eve wedding. That means there's lots of planning to be done, but I don't know if you heard how busy the happy couple is, so Fi asked me to help plan it all and suggested we work together so that's how I got your email. What do you say, want to help me make their wedding dreams come true?

From: bo@grantandco.com
To: izzydoesbooks@mymail.com

Subject: Re: Fiona and Louie

Dear Izzy,

I would do anything for Louie, so I guess you can count me in. But I do work long hours and I am in New York, so we'll have to stick to email. I can have my assistant Mirna make calls for us. Send me over whatever you need.

Sincerely,
Bo Grant

From: izzydoesbooks@mymail.com
To: bo@grantandco.com
Subject: Re: Fiona and Louie

Dearest Bo,

Your assistant? No, no, no, that won't do. If this wedding is going to be special, it needs to be planned at the hands of people who know Fiona and Louie. I know you don't get the whole love thing, but this needs to be about love, planned with love and for love. See what I'm saying?

Izzy Monroe

P.S. Sorry, but this whole formal email thing seems a little stuffy. We're going to be friends-in-law soon, so maybe we can act like it.

From: bo@grantandco.com
To: izzydoesbooks@mymail.com
Subject: Re: Fiona and Louie

Izzy,

Friends-in-law? What is that? Have you been drinking?

Sincerely,
Bo Grant

From: izzydoesbooks@mymail.com
To: bo@grantandco.com
Subject: Fiona and Louie

Oh, Bo, you're funny. You know what I mean. So do you want to handle the contracts with the vendors? I have several that need to be looked over. That seems right up your alley. What do you say?

From: bo@grantandco.com
To: izzydoesbooks@mymail.com
Subject: Re: Fiona and Louie

That I can do. Send them over.

From: izzydoesbooks@mymail.com
To: bo@grantandco.com
Subject: Next

You dropped the formalities in our last email... I noticed!
All the contracts have been returned; thanks for your help.

The venue is handling rentals and Fi already has her dress.
Louie's back in town next week and will be going for a
fitting. Do you need a fitting? You should get that done. The
attire is important, you know. We want to make sure
everyone looks good for the pictures.

From: bo@grantandco.com
To: izzydoesbooks@mymail.com
Subject: Re: Next

Did I ever give you reason to believe I thought attire wasn't
important no matter the occasion? Maybe you forgot but

when we met at the bar I was wearing nice, clean cut jeans and a buttoned down shirt. You can take a deep breath, I have my suit already fitted and hanging in my closet. Are we done with the planning now?

Bo
P.S. I can be informal, too.

From: izzydoesbooks@mymail.com
To: bo@grantandco.com
Subject: Wedding planning is never done

Are we done? Ha! See how I changed the subject... now you won't forget. Let's see, consulting my handy wedding planning checklist... we're doing good. Honeymoon's booked already. They have an officiant. Save-the-dates went out. You got yours, right?

From: bo@grantandco.com
To: izzydoesbooks@mymail.com
Subject: Re: Wedding planning is never done

Of course. You do know I have actual work to do, so maybe you can just tell me what you need from me?

From: bo@grantandco.com
To: izzydoesbooks@mymail.com
Subject: Re: Wedding planning is never done

You know what, I had Mirna get me a checklist, too. So now I know what's up. Let me ask you, have you sent out invitations? I didn't get mine in the mail yet. Have they written their vows?

I can ask questions, too!

From: izzydoesbooks@mymail.com
To: bo@grantandco.com
Subject: Re: Wedding planning is never done

You know when we met I doubted this, but you're proving to be a fun one, Mr. Grant. Yes, those things are all accounted for. You should see your invitation in the mail any day now. We need to start brainstorming favors and gift bags. Then when you get here we can put them together. When exactly will you be coming into town?

From: bo@grantandco.com
To: izzydoesbooks@mymail.com
Subject: Re: Wedding planning is never done

My assistant is looking at my calendar now, so I'll get back to you on that. Remember, I work, as I explained. As for favors I'm good with anything. Louie likes those little bottles of alcohol whenever he travels, says they make him feel like a giant. Maybe we can get those?

———————————————

From: izzydoesbooks@mymail.com
To: bo@grantandco.com
Subject: Re: Wedding planning is never done

First of all, it's the holiday season, surely, you can get away from the office. No one does business this late in the game. Second, we cannot give out little bottles of alcohol as you put it. They need to be selected with love and care. How about seed packets?

———————————————

From: bo@grantandco.com
To: izzydoesbooks@mymail.com
Subject: Re: Wedding planning is never done

So people can grow their own love? Hey, that's not a bad idea. Here, my assistant found a few, I'm attaching pictures.

By the way, the corporate world never sleeps. Holidays included.

From: izzydoesbooks@mymail.com
To: bo@grantandco.com
Subject: Playlists

I ordered the favors. Thank Mirna for me for finding them. She's good. You should give her a raise. Next: playlists. We have to give the DJ song ideas for the five big moments. We also have to give him a do-not-play list. I'll await song ideas for both lists.

———————————————

From: bo@grantandco.com
To: izzydoesbooks@mymail.com
Subject: Re: Playlists

You do know I'm a man, right? I don't speak wedding. What are the five big moments?

———————————————

From: izzydoesbooks@mymail.com
To: bo@grantandco.com
Subectj: Re: Playlists

Forget it. I took care of it. Maybe I even asked the DJ to give us a karaoke moment so we can relive the last time you were in town and you can actually sing this time. Kidding, you can relax! Now, speaking of, we just need to get you into town. When will you be arriving? I can pick you up from the airport... I assume you're flying in. Send me the details.

———————————————

From: bo@grantandco.com
To: izzydoesbooks@mymail.com
Subject: Re: Playlists

No, thanks. I'll handle my own transportation. I'll be coming into town sometime next week and we've cleared my schedule through the end of the year. I figured besides the wedding, it'll be my big vacation this year since I haven't taken one yet.

———————————————

From: izzydoesbooks@mymail.com
To: bo@grantandco.com
Subject: Re: Playlists

Never would I have guessed you'd see coming to our little town as a vacation. Lucky us, you're gracing us with your presence for quite a while. I'll be sure to inform the town crier so your arrival can herald in the season. I really don't mind picking you up, we can talk about the wedding, so just send me the details if you change your mind.

From: bo@grantandco.com
To: izzydoesbooks@mymail.com
Subject: Re: Playlists

Don't get me wrong, it's not my idea of a vacation, but it can never be said I'm a lousy friend. As for you picking me up, really, it's okay. I enjoy my quiet time. I'll call you once I've settled in. And please don't ask where I'm staying, I do like my peace and quiet, as I said. Remember, this is part vacation for me.

Sincerest regards,
Bo Grant

Chapter Three

Bo

THE PRESENT

I looked into the rearview mirror and Santa, er, Jesse something-or-other, caught my eye. Averting his gaze, I looked down again. I already knew why he was dressed like Santa—apparently, he was going to the children's hospital after dropping me off—but what I couldn't figure out was what made this man so happy.

Did the townspeople here always look this happy? Sure, the last time I was here I learned these people had more pep in their step than people in the city, but this was next level. I'd been looking out the window on our short drive from the train station, and every single person I saw walking around had a smile on their face.

Yeah, it was Christmastime, but was that any reason to be *this* jolly? If anything, I'd swear it was the exact opposite. The reason of all reasons to be, well, unhappy. I shook my head, decidedly not interested in knowing what was up with these people and turned my attention back to the article I was reading online.

It was about me.

Naturally.

And it made my skin crawl.

Again, naturally.

Just listen to this line: "When Bo walked into the room, there was a chill that ran through the air and as his dark brown eyes met mine, it was obvious he was a man who demanded attention. Like no matter what he did, there was no way he could be identified as a wallflower."

Sure, I voluntarily went along with the interview—and by voluntarily, I meant was all but forced into it by my father —but sitting down to talk with some writer for a blog was never my idea of good press. I believed good press were the pieces that were picked up discussing the good we were doing as a company, not talking about me. No, that was never good in my opinion. But my father felt differently.

Anyway, if you thought that was bad, just get a load of the rest of it: "Indeed, Bo Grant possessed the same great presence as his father, Robert Grant, who I had the distinct pleasure of meeting a few months ago at a charity event. Bo had the same looks as his father, the same unruly dark brown hair, and strong jawline. Only, Bo's full beard gave him an edge his father didn't have.

"It's no surprise this man is about to take over one of the biggest conglomerates in New York City. Remember, you read it here first: Robert Grant is retiring in the new year and Bo Grant, his only heir, is taking over. The company will still hold the respectable Grant & Co. name but will have a new generation at the helm.

"When asked if he's ready to take on such a responsibility, Bo commented, 'It's what I've been working toward my whole life.' Needless to say, this handsome man is about to become the Big Apple's most eligible bachelor. Don't send your letters to Santa quite yet, ladies, because this sexy man is going to need a woman and if you've been nice, maybe Christmas will come early for you."

What did that even mean?

I closed the screen on my phone and flipped it over on the seat next to me, not able to look at it anymore. I couldn't read another word of it. Wasn't it bad enough that I was here in Silver Springs, North Carolina, population of—*oh, what was it again?*—about sixteen hundred, at Christmastime, for my friend's wedding? And now my assistant had to send me all the links to articles I'd been featured in? Who in their right mind wanted to read about themselves like that?

Certainly not me. I exhaled and closed my eyes, my head leaning back against the headrest.

Besides, didn't Mirna remember I was on a vacation? I was taking the last break I'd be afforded before the new year when I stepped into my role as CEO and I was supposed to be helping my best friend—my only friend, Louie—get married.

How much longer until we got where we were going, I wondered.

"So what brings you to Silver Springs?" Jesse asked casually, interrupting my thoughts.

It occurred to me that I could say I was here just 'cause. Or for a good time. But what made it a good time, really? The musty, exhaust-filled smell of his old jalopy? The fact that more people lived on my block in New York City than in this town? Nope, I couldn't say any of that.

I raised a brow when my eyes came across a half-eaten bag of potato chips sitting on his dashboard. "Personal reasons," I answered simply, not sure I wanted to say more. What business was it of his anyway?

Not that he probably didn't already know about the wedding. I had a feeling the whole town knew. Heck, they were probably all invited. But I still wasn't divulging.

He gave me a weak shrug and went on driving with one hand on the wheel as he brushed his fingers through his long, white beard that would impress a mountain man. I was all for facial hair—if a man could grow it out, then he should. I mean, just look at me, I had a beard of my own. But there was also such a thing as too long and thick, like when-a-crumb-falls-and-you-can't-find-it-for-a-few-days long. That was how Jesse's beard was. And it wasn't a rental that came with the Santa suit.

"You sticking around for the tree lighting?" Jesse tried again to make conversation, cranking his window down and placing one red velvet-clad arm out the side of the car.

I rubbed the back of my neck and hoped this ride would be over sometime soon, preferably before I pulled my hair out. "There's a tree lighting?" Who was I kidding, of course there was.

"It's been going on for as far back as I can remember. Way before I came into town when I was just about your age." Then he paused before questioning, "How old are you?"

I fought the urge to groan. I was in no physical pain, so the groan would probably be unnecessary, but talking about the holidays was painful enough to warrant it. I also leaned my elbow on the window, realizing it was probably better to engage in this idle chit-chat than wait for him to come to a stop. "Thirty-two."

He nodded. "Yeah, I was about your age when I came to town." Then he guffawed. "You know, there are lots of ladies in this town about your age. Single, in fact, and would jump at the chance to be with a big city slicker like yourself."

Great, and I was here for a wedding and everyone knew what that meant—single women looking for a date.

How I desperately hoped he was wrong. My mind suddenly started reeling with images of women standing in line for a sale on meat, only I was the meat being served up. That was a nightmare I didn't want to think about for another second. "Oh," I said, "I doubt that." I'd learned a long time ago that women just didn't migrate to me the same way they did other men. It hurt when it first hit home, but I'd learned quick enough that I was just fine with that.

I rolled up my shirtsleeves. While it may have been below fifty degrees out there, in this old beaten-down car it was starting to feel stifling. "Anyway, about this tree lighting," I started, hoping he'd pick up that thread again.

Turned out between talk of Christmas and dating, I chose the former.

Yeah, even I was surprised by that one.

"You should make sure to stick around for it," Jesse said, nodding his head like a bobblehead, his eyes on me in the rearview mirror again.

He should only know I didn't think I had much choice in the matter. The wedding was Christmas Eve, so I'd be here for it all. Unfortunately.

I shrugged my shoulders. "Definitely, looking forward to it," I lied. "But if I had it my way, I wouldn't be here more than the day," I mumbled under my breath.

Jesse shook his head and began rolling to a stop. "Why do I get the sense you're not?" Then he clarified, "Looking forward to it, that is. You look like you could use a little Christmas spirit."

Man, I knew there was something I forgot to pack. That was right, I left my jar of Christmas spirit on my dresser. Geez, next time I'd have to be more mindful about carrying it with me.

"I'm good, thanks." When he came to a complete stop, I furrowed my brows. This wasn't the bed and breakfast where I was staying. "Why are we stopping in front of a coffee shop?" I looked at my watch. I was hoping to check in before Izzy got wind of me being in town. Once she heard, I had a feeling I wouldn't get any peace. She was like Ms. Wedding and I could only handle her in small doses.

He shut off the car, but left the key in the ignition and opened the door, got out, then went to close it behind him.

"Um, you left the key in the car," I alerted him quickly.

He waved his hand in the air as he shut the door, as though to say no big deal. Where I came from it was a huge deal, but if he wanted to be so careless, then that was his problem, not mine.

I opened the door and shouted, "You never answered my question."

"Thought it was obvious," he jested, knocking on the roof. "I'm going to get a special cup o' Joe."

"Now? I thought you were driving me to the bed and breakfast and you had somewhere to be." I got out of the car and slammed the door shut behind me. That was when I read the sign outside the shop and saw they were offering gingerbread lattes. "Is that what we're here for?" I asked, pointing to the sign.

He nodded.

"You can't get that after you drop me off?"

"No can do. They're only serving them up for a limited time and only in the morning hours. That means every morning until Christmas I'll be here ordering myself a gingerbread latte."

Was this man for real? Before I could say another word, he was opening the door and heading in. *Great, just great.*

"Might as well order a cup of coffee," I muttered to no one in particular, cursing the fact that I let myself get dragged into this situation where I had to be in this town straight out of a Christmas card.

Thank you, Louie.

I opened the door when I heard teeth chattering behind me. A young girl, no older than sixteen, came up to the side of me. "Do you mind?" she asked, smiling, as she pointed to the door and looking to see if I would let her go in first.

I tilted my head toward the door, allowing her entry and watched her walk in, taking off her scarf as she did, and sighing heavily. Maybe she was new in town because it was close enough to the mountains that this place, I imagined, got pretty chilly this time of year.

"Thank you," she said over her shoulder, her voice filled with joy. *More joy. Ugh.*

I'd have thought it was joy for the fact that she was finally in a warm setting, but she was smiling even when her teeth were chattering and she was obviously chillier than she cared to be. It was like everyone in this blasted town had an aversion to real emotion—aside from happiness, that was.

Everything was a reason for these people to smile, even something as silly as gingerbread lattes. Not that I would ever know what that was about, because when I got to the counter I ordered my usual—coffee, black. Personally, I didn't see the appeal to add all that nonsense to my coffee. It made it less coffee and more like a child's drink, especially with all that sugar. Even when I was a child I didn't consume that many sweets. Quite frankly, maybe that was the source of their problem—endless sugar highs.

"Will that be all, sir?"

I watched as the woman tossed her long blonde hair over her shoulder and moved to the pot behind her, filling up a cup for me.

"That's all," I finally answered, stuffing my hands in my pockets, and looking around as I waited. Everyone seemed to be talking to someone, and I didn't see Jesse anywhere. Not that he could be missed dressed as he was.

With my focus on finding Jesse so we could get the heck out of here, I almost missed my cup of coffee being placed on the counter. Until the only sweet as saccharine voice I knew filled my ears and stepped up to me, holding the to-go cup out for me to take. "I think this is yours," she said with, what else, but a smile on her face.

Izzy Monroe.

The maid of honor to my best man.

My emailing, um, buddy.

The woman who drove me up a wall.

I grinned, eyeing the mysterious candy cane that seemed to have been added to my cup. On second thought, I said, "I don't think that's mine."

The truth was, just like the first time I'd met her, my eyes couldn't seem to leave the brown ones that were currently staring into mine. They sparkled with more hope than I cared for in a person. Her long brown hair was tied in some criss-crossed style off to the side of her head and draped over her shoulder.

With one hand around the cup she was forcing on me and the other holding the front of her blue coat, she nudged me again. "I think it is. No one else here drinks black coffee." *Of course they didn't.* "Now, why didn't you tell me you were in town?" she asked suddenly, her voice going up a few octaves.

I shook my head. "I didn't?"

She hitched an eyebrow in the air and waited. "I believe your last email said sometime next week."

"I just got in," I conceded. "I didn't want to impose. I was going to call you later."

What? It was true. Well, if later meant never.

Don't judge me. If you met Izzy and spent five seconds around her ray-of-sunshine-personality, you would understand my aversion to spending too much time with her. Okay, fine, any time at all.

I reached for my cup in hopes of ending this conversation and finding Jesse once and for all. Before turning to leave, I plucked the candy cane from my coffee, not sure what to do with it. Didn't anyone here appreciate plain coffee? "What is with this town?" I asked no one in particular.

Izzy answered, though, in a rather sing-song voice. "It is the holiday season. Candy canes come with the territory."

"In my black coffee?" It felt a little disrespectful to the bean.

She rolled back on her heels and winked. "Especially in your black coffee. You need something to help that bitter stuff."

"I like it bitter, thank you very much."

Izzy quirked a brow, as though daring me to think differently. I was going to do no such thing. Then, without preamble, she said, "I have a feeling you'll be changing your tune soon enough."

I began moving away from her and toward the door. Apparently, even without an invitation, she decided to follow me. *Fine, I'd bite.* "What do you want?" Wasn't it a little soon to be talking about Fiona and Louie's wedding? I took a sip of my coffee, all while holding the stupid, sticky candy cane in my hand.

She rolled her eyes and snagged the treat from me, bringing the hook to her mouth and popping it off in one swift motion.

Dumbfounded, I stared at her. "What are you doing?"

"Mmm," she moaned sucking on it. "Delicious." Then she waved the rest of the stick as she spoke, the whole thing oddly reminiscent of my elementary school teacher using a finger pointer. "You didn't know what to do with it and let's be honest, we both know you were going to throw it away. I couldn't possibly let a perfectly good candy cane go to waste."

"Naturally," I replied, sarcasm dripping from that one word. "So what is it you wanted?" I asked again, still wondering why she was following.

She cracked down on the candy cane in her mouth, the crunching on her teeth actually concerning to my ears. "I know you said this was part wedding, part vacation for you, but I was wondering how long you needed to settle in before we got down to business on the wedding details. You know, Fiona's been in court and her trial doesn't seem to be ending anytime soon. So we can't fail her now. She needs all the help she can get, and Louie's still traveling, so he's rarely here for longer than a day or two before leaving again. It's his busy season," she reminded me unnecessarily.

Yeah, Louie—the lucky fellow he was—was in tech and he was working on some big projects before the new year. Too bad I had to work in corporate when everything all but shut down, leaving time for me to help with planning his and Fiona's wedding with Ms. Cheerful, er, Wedding. She was Ms. A Lot of Things.

As she waited for me to answer, she popped the candy cane in her mouth, and placed a finger in the air. She took her hair down out of the style she had it in, and then continued to pull a thicker band than the one that was in her hair previously out of the bag on her shoulder and began wrapping her hair in it until it was tied tightly on the top of her head.

"Sorry," she said, "sometimes it just bugs me being on my shoulder."

I rather liked it down actually, I immediately thought. Wait, why did I care the way she wore her hair?

It was this town. I was starting to lose it.

Shaking my head, I addressed her question, noting, "Yeah, I know. I'd like to just get to my room and put my luggage down and then I'll call you." I hoped that was enough to get her off my back for the time being.

She sighed. "Works for me."

"Don't you have work?" I asked, looking at my watch.

"No," she said, shaking her head. "I own the bookstore, so I come and go as I please."

That explained her email address. I nodded my understanding. "Well, you should do whatever you were planning on doing with the day." Then in the ultimate moment of good fortune, I spotted Jesse walking from across the street. "Well, it looks like my ride is here," I said, cutting our conversation short.

She rolled her eyes and took a bite of the candy cane again. "I'll be waiting, Bo."

The way she said that gave me chills.

I was actually afraid to have to spend any significant time with her.

Louie definitely owed me for this one because I may not have known much about her, but I did know this: working with this Izzy character was going to be a real treat (sense the sarcasm).

Here was what I did know from these ever so brief encounters: she was excited about most things, she smiled incessantly (let's just assume unless I say otherwise everyone is smiling), she liked books, and apparently she was the queen of organization and loved planning big events like weddings. I only hoped that was where it ended and I didn't get to know more about her, because if I did, that meant we were spending way too much time together. I mean, I knew that being in the wedding party, we'd be thrown together, but come on.

And maybe that made me out to be some kind of beast, but at least I was honest.

* * *

I looked out the window like before and tried my best to tune out the Christmas music Jesse put on. I didn't get what the stink was with the holidays. They claimed it was the happiest time of the year. Some people wished it would be year-round. Whereas, I wished it could be erased off the calendar all together.

Christmas was never a joyous occasion when I was growing up.

My grandmother was really the only one who took the time to make the holidays special for me, but she passed when I was young, and she took all the good times with her.

My parents didn't care much for decorating, considering it too much work for one day. We didn't have stockings and they didn't even give me a chance to believe in Santa Claus.

They never bothered wrapping my presents, just gave them to me as they were. "Here you go, Bo," my mother would say, shoving the gift in my hands. "From your father and I. We hope you like it."

And come Christmas Day, for dinner we would go to a fancy restaurant in the city to eat, just as we did every year. I guessed you could say it was our tradition. I called it just another day, only this night my parents insisted I wear a scratchy sweater.

I attended a private, non-denominational school that didn't celebrate the holidays, either. The most we ever did was make paper snowflakes. I brought mine home one year and hung it on my wall, only for my father to take it down and say that it didn't go with the statement he and my mother were trying to make.

The Grants couldn't afford to look like anything but the perfect, socialite, upper-class family we were. Apparently, even when it came to my bedroom decor.

That was why the holidays were no big deal, in my opinion. It was merely another day where childrens' heads were filled with promises that would likely never be fulfilled and lies that would crumble around them when they were old enough to fully grapple with the truth. The truth being, of course, that like Valentine's Day, Christmas was just another day that wasn't worth the time or money spent on the wrapping paper for the gifts, let alone the gifts themselves.

When we pulled up in front of the bed and breakfast—Holly's Haven—I almost cringed at the way it was decked out to the nines in holiday decor. Even the sign was framed in lights.

"This is it. Have a good stay," Jesse said, tapping his fingers on the steering wheel as he came to a stop.

"Yeah. Thanks for the ride." I got out, went around to the back and got my things out of the trunk. Still hardly believing that in all that time we were parked outside the coffee shop no one stole my bags. I was learning there were definitely differences between living in the city and being in a small town. There wasn't much I liked about being here, but being able to trust your neighbor seemed like a nice bonus.

By the time I started walking to the front door, I heard his car pull away. Don't get me wrong, Jesse was a nice guy, but if I never smelled the smells of his car again, it'd be too soon.

I took a second before opening the door and looked around at my surroundings. Besides all the lights, there was a tree in the yard, garland, well, everywhere, red bows and plastic snowmen. I actually shuddered at the prospect that the inside of this place might look more festive than this.

There was a jingling sound from the bells moving on the wreath outside the door as I went in and shut the door behind me, leaving the chilly air outside. My feet immediately sank down on a plush dark green rug that had more fur than a cat. The rug read "Ho-Ho-Ho" and had a Santa hat hanging off the first H.

As I continued walking with my suitcase rolling behind me and my suit in the garment bag hung over my arm, the lady behind the desk with striking red hair and an elf hat on greeted me. "I hope this weather isn't too much for you, dear."

I shook my head. "It's fine. I'm from New York so," I let my words fall off, hoping that was all the explanation she needed.

"Say no more," she said, the words music to my ears. "You're Bo Grant, right?"

Of course she knew. "My assistant made a reservation for me."

"Yes, I remember. I'm Holly, by the way." She held up a finger, bent down, and grabbed a key, extending a hand out for me to take the room key. "You're in our Snow Globe Room."

I gave her a dumbfounded look, tilting my head. "What does that mean exactly?"

She chuckled, clearly amused by my lack of knowledge on the way she organized this place. "It just means that snow globes are the theme for that room. Every room has a theme for the holidays. Helps make it more festive for the guests."

I wasn't going to touch that one with a 10-foot pole. "All right, well, I guess I'll be on my way, then."

She stopped me as I walked past the desk, touching my shoulder to get my attention. "I hear you're in town for Louie and Fiona's wedding."

I nodded. So the small town lore rang true—gossip was alive and well. Apparently, Jesse wasn't on the gossip circuit, but Holly was.

"Izzy says you've been helping her plan the thing since the lovebirds are so busy with work. Mighty kind of you, you know."

Kind wasn't a word often used to describe me, as you could tell from that article I read on the way over here. "Thanks. I should really be going," I said, not wanting to make any more small talk. "I have, um, planning to do and work to get caught up on."

She blinked and nodded. "Very well. I hope to see you around."

"Sure."

I followed the room numbers and walked to my room, noticing that the Gingerbread Room and Elf Room were on either side of mine. I honestly didn't know which was worse, but was beginning to thank my lucky stars that I got the Snow Globe Room because obviously that was the lesser of the evils.

I flicked a cranberry that was hanging from the holly around the door. "I have to get out of here," I whispered to myself, taking the room key out and going to open the door. "And fast," I spoke low, practically under my breath, as I pushed in.

I couldn't help but wonder what Mirna was thinking when she booked me at the B&B. I knew it was a small town and all, but why exactly couldn't I stay at the same hotel I stayed in last time I was here and commute back and forth? I almost kicked myself for authorizing that huge bonus because this was all her fault. It was because of Mirna that I was subjected to all this Christmas nonsense.

"You have got to be kidding me," I said under my breath, taking it all in. It was just so much Christmas. Being in my room alone was like visiting the North Pole—if such a place existed, that was.

There was a shelf off to the corner filled with snow globes, so that obviously explained that, but everything else seemed a bit too much, if you asked me. Almost like it was taken straight out of a scene from a Christmas movie. I didn't even want to watch them, let alone live out one. How was I supposed to get any sleep, though, when there was a giant nutcracker sitting beside the door staring at me? Or better yet, the giant snow globe shaped pillow sitting on the middle of the bed.

I left my suitcase and garment bag at the door and walked over to the desk that had fake snow covering it. There was even a big red chair that looked like it belonged to Santa Claus. Draped across the back of it was a Santa costume. Clearly, that was in the wrong room. There must have been a Santa Room or something that was missing a key decoration.

Draped on the curtains were paper snowflakes like the ones I made when I was a boy and I couldn't help but look at them with disdain. This place was going to be the death of me.

I walked over and pulled back the curtains to find snow globe decals cluttering the window and fake snow littering the windowsill. There was no escaping it, was there?

Admitting defeat, I sat on the edge of the bed. There was nothing I could do about it now. I was here for Louie, I just had to keep reminding myself that.

I placed a hand down beside me on the bed, and immediately looked down at the plush quilt on it. It was light blue and covered in snow and snowflakes. "Of course."

This was absurd.

It wasn't possible that these people couldn't see that this wasn't real. That Christmas wasn't anything special.

I raked a hand through my hair before resting my elbows on my knees and leaning forward. I glanced around the room one more time before staring up at the ceiling. "I hate the holidays," I repeated to myself, not for the first time today. This was just the first time I was saying it aloud.

Chapter Four

Izzy

"Izzy, I know I'll have you seeing things my way soon enough." Gavin crossed his arms and leaned back against a short white bookshelf off to the side, so he could be at the best angle to watch me as I finished stocking the new shipment of romance books that just came in.

Did he help? No.

Watch? Yes.

Did that do me any good? Not really.

But, honestly, I just wanted him to leave.

Gavin Clarke was a real estate agent in town, the best one we had, and he was—*what was the word for it?*—cocky. It was like he knew how handsome he was and thought everyone should treat him like gold because of it. Huge superiority complex, if you asked me.

Let me explain how we got to this place, though, him standing in my bookstore, pestering me for the hundredth time to go out on a date with him. I didn't think we were compatible. Heck, I knew we weren't. He was so. . . and I was so. . . . It just wouldn't work.

He cleared his throat and I looked to him and watched him scratch his chin as he checked me out, literally staring me up and down.

What the women in town told me: "You should feel so lucky"; "I wish Gavin would look at me like that"; "You should give him a chance"; "He's one fine man."

What I'd been told they said behind my back: "Foolish girl"; "She'll never meet anyone as great as Gavin"; "Izzy is too busy with those silly romance novels to see what's right in front of her."

But I didn't care. I liked to think I'd know when I met my dream man, and news flash: I hadn't found him yet. And it certainly wasn't a man like Gavin Clarke.

I tried hard not to roll my eyes, and blew a strand of brown hair out of my eye. I placed it in a loose bun, but had a feeling it was becoming *too* loose because it was starting to fall. Finally, I responded, "Gavin, that's never going to happen. I'm just not interested."

He guffawed and in a deep voice reiterated in a questioning tone, "Not interested? But, Izzy, I can have any girl in this town and I'm choosing to spend one evening with you."

Oof, laying it on thick, weren't we?

"Lucky me, but you'll have to ask one of those other girls out because I don't think this is going to become a thing." With my hands finally free of the last book I had in them before having to move onto the next stack, I took my hair down and quickly retied it back in another bun. "Like I've said many times before," I added for good measure.

"Okay, not dinner, then. How about coffee? You have to stop at the coffee shop at some point. I'll run into you there and we'll sit down and chat."

I sighed as I bent down and grabbed another stack of books from the floor. "No." *What did they say about throwing a dog a bone?* "But I will be here when Santa reads to the children and wouldn't say no to the company."

As though a lightbulb went off, he snapped his fingers and widened his dark brown eyes. "That's brilliant. I'll be there." Then he pushed away from the shelf and walked over to me, helping me off the floor. His eyes staring into mine, he looked serious as he rested his hands on my shoulders. "You won't regret this. And after that date, we'll have another one. I'll make you dinner. I make a mean lobster ragu."

I glanced at his hands on me.

Chuckling, he backed away and started toward the door. Walking backward as he spoke, he pointed a finger in my direction. "Oh, Izzy, this is all I've ever wanted." He continued backing up right into one of my best customers coming in the store with her niece.

"Uh," Stassia announced, and Gavin had the decency to stop walking backward and apologize. "Watch where you're walking, Gavin. You could've knocked into my niece."

Gavin plastered a wide smile on his face, all of his white teeth on full display. I imagined a sparkle would appear like in those cartoons. "Stassia," he tried smooth-talking her now. "You really should try and relax a little."

Stassia rolled her eyes and grabbed hold of Mackenzie's hand. "Weren't you leaving?"

Ah, yes, one of the things I liked most about Stassia was that she was the only—and I mean the only—person in my camp against Gavin. Not that I was against him, I just wasn't all for him like everyone else in this town was.

"Yes, I was," he answered, glaring over his shoulder at me and winking. "See you soon, Izzy."

When he was finally gone and the door closed behind him, I let out a deep breath I didn't know I was holding.

Practically shuddering, Stassia let go of Mackenzie's hand and told me, "I don't like that guy." She turned around and looked at the door like he might come back. He wouldn't. He already got what he wanted—a date with me. Not that it was a date by any standards, but in his head, I knew it was. He wouldn't show his face again until the day of the Christmas reading.

The truth was, he was so full of himself that he didn't think he needed to woo me because he felt he already had me. It was just how men like him were. Believe me, I'd been dealing with the likes of Gavin since he moved here a year ago.

I chuckled. "I know." With books in hand, I made my way to the counter and stood behind it, placing them down. "He asked me out. Again," I tacked on to the end. Although, I didn't know why. Everyone in this town knew he wasn't one to give up and he had his sights set on me.

It was like most of the town was under Gavin's spell or something. "No one was as handsome as Gavin"; "No one was as muscular as Gavin." They all traveled in packs and like moths to a flame were drawn to him.

"Auntie, can I look around?" Mackenzie asked, her bouncy red curls moving around as she rocked on her feet, clearly excited to shop for new books.

Stassia was sister to Dru, who worked long hours at her job as a nurse at the hospital (she was trying to be a good person—at least that was the story I was always told), so Stassia stepped up and helped out as much as she could. And luckily for me, Mackenzie was an avid reader. The little girl reminded me of myself when I was her age. That was when it all started for me—my love for books. "Sure," she answered, letting her go, then she leaned forward and eyed me. "So what does he want this time?"

I placed an elbow on the counter and shrugged my shoulders. "What else? And I gave in. Somewhat."

"What?" she shrieked and then reeled it in, practically whispering now. "What?" she repeated even though she didn't need to. I got that she was shocked the first time. "You don't actually mean—" She tried again, "You didn't actually —" She smacked her lips together and closed her eyes. "Nope. I can't even get the words out. They're, like, vile."

I raked my teeth over my bottom lip. "To answer the question you can't bring yourself to ask, yes, I did."

"You're not actually going out with that. . . that arrogant, uncultured swine, are you?" she asked, her eyes like saucers.

Even to my own ears, it sounded a little unbelievable. I'd been fending him off for so long, but even I had to cave at some point. "Stassia!" I admonished. Sometimes, she could be downright wicked with her words. Don't get me wrong, I liked her, but she needed a filter.

"Sorry, but he's just so—"

"I know," I supplied, trying to be less surprised. "It's not really a date," I explained, "it's more like a meeting. Here at the bookstore. I invited him to come to Santa's reading."

Shaking her head, she started helping me move books to reorganize the shelves. I was setting up a Christmas display of all the holiday books. Romance in the front, of course, and children's books off to the side. All the other genres would be around the other side. "At least you'll have an audience. I swear, he gives me the creeps," she said, practically shuddering. "Anyway, rumor has it Louie's friend, Bo Grant, is in town," Stassia noted. "He's like a New York billionaire, you know."

I finished what I was doing at the display and moved around the back to start working alongside Stassia. "I didn't."

"You need to read the Internet more often. Blogs. They are full of information, not like in your books, but modern information."

I looked up and over at her. "Har! Har! I'm busy. So tell me, what's his deal?"

"He's taking over his father's company in the new year. The man is like the most eligible bachelor of the decade. And since you'll be working with him on the wedding, you should try to feel him out. Maybe—"

I put my hand up to stop her right there. "He may be the most eligible bachelor, but he's also too grumpy for my liking. And I try with him, I really do, but he just doesn't get it. Like with the wedding, he has a whole different approach."

Stassia shrugged. "Big deal."

"I don't know, Bo's not an overly talkative person. He doesn't share much about himself." Then I corrected, "He doesn't share much in general, actually. I can't see him looking for a romantic entanglement."

"You've been reading way too many of those romance books you love so much."

I waved the last book in my hand at her. "Whatever." No one ever understood my love of books. The way they fed my soul. The way they gave me something to hope for, dream about. It was like I could actually believe in this great big universe and all that was out there, love included. Books had this way of showing me the world, period. But I was tired of explaining that, so I changed the subject. "The wedding planning is going great."

"How's Fiona's trial?"

I shrugged. "It has her so tied up. I'd be a nervous wreck this close to my wedding if I were her. I mean, not being able to think about it or plan for it." *I couldn't even imagine.*

"For my wedding, I decided I don't want a big to-do. Instead, I'm thinking we'll elope or maybe go away somewhere and elope. Even better."

"But your mother," I reminded her. Wouldn't she want her mother there? I knew they weren't the closest, and her mother might've done some less than savory things, but it must've came from a place of love. Right?

She picked up one of the books she just set out on the display and flipped through the pages. "One of the benefits to eloping. To do it far from Mother."

Just then Mackenzie ran up to us, clutching two books to her chest. "Auntie, I can't decide, can I buy both?"

"Sure, sweetie. Just make it fast, we have to get you to the vet to pick up Grandma's cat before they close."

I led them to the checkout counter and bagged her new books so Stassia wouldn't be late. I knew that cat and he wasn't named Spike for no reason. Surely, he wouldn't take kindly to being left, and his claws would come out as soon as he was out of the office. I'd bet my life on it.

"Thanks for helping me."

"Thanks for talking with me," Stassia said, smiling. "See you next week." She took Mackenzie's hand and led her out of the store.

With the place quiet again, I looked around and realized I was happy with the displays. I just needed to add a few more decorations before Santa arrived and I'd be all set.

That meant one thing. I could try to get some wedding planning in for Fiona.

That meant getting ahold of Bo.

I picked up my phone and shot an email to him since I had no idea where he was staying.

From: izzydoesbooks@mymail.com
To: bo@grantandco.com
Subject: In town

Hi, Bo. Since you're in town maybe we can get the cake picked out if you have the time. Let me know. I can call Phoebe and get us in for a tasting. -Izzy

Chapter Five

Bo

"Knock, knock."

I looked up from my laptop where I was settled on the chair by the window and knew Holly's voice when I heard it.

"It's open." After breakfast, I didn't think I ever locked it again, which by the way was its own form of torture. I wouldn't bother boring you with all the details, but let's just say I didn't think I was cut out for staying at a bed and breakfast. At least not in a small town where the gossip mill ran faster than Louie when he was being chased by a great dane back in college.

As Holly entered, I had to actually stop my eyes from bulging out of my head like a cartoon character when I caught sight of what she was wearing.

An ugly Christmas sweater.

At least, that was what I thought it was, since there was a reindeer's head quite literally coming out the front of it. There was three-dimensional and then there was this thing. Why on earth would someone wear something that. . . horrific? Let alone purchase it to begin with.

I knew one thing for sure—if someone gifted that thing to me, it would go straight to the back of my closet never to be seen again. I wouldn't even regift it, that would just be harsh. I didn't hate anyone enough. Maybe I would toss it right in the incinerator, that sounded like a much better idea.

"I come bearing gifts," she said, bringing the hand she had behind her back to the front of her and showing off a small tree. "I always make it a point to put one in each of the guests' rooms around this time." She twirled it around like I had never seen a fake tree before and let out a happy sigh as she smiled. "Isn't it the cutest?"

I scratched my chin and searched for the right words. "It's something," I finally settled on.

Clearly not paying a bit of attention to the fact that I wanted no part in that thing, she continued, "I just love decorating for the holidays. It's one of my favorite parts of owning my own place with so many rooms. There's so much space to decorate."

That was one way to put it. Call me boring, but I much preferred to leave the place the way it came—clean, free of clutter.

"I leave them undecorated, though, so if the guests want to, they can decorate it themselves. Add their own fun spin on it, you know?"

I cocked a brow and stared at it like it was Medusa's head. "Yeah, I'm not much for the holidays, so I probably won't be decorating that, but I appreciate you bringing it by."

What did no one understand about this concept? Some people—okay, not these people, but some people—just didn't enjoy this time of year. Just because I was here in this town of Christmas lovers, didn't mean I would become one of them.

Yeah, that was right—Christmas lovers.

Christmas connoisseurs.

If Christmas was a person, they would kiss them senseless, take them in their arms and hold onto them for dear life.

Christmas equated to a four letter word for these people —l-o-v-e.

"So you've said." She placed it on the table by the window and draped the white cotton she had already down around it. "But you might find that being here might just change the way you see the holidays, Bo." Before leaving, she pointed to the tree. "And try to decorate it, if you could, you don't want it to look all sad, do you?"

Can a tree look sad? I looked over at it and tilted my head thinking about her words. "Maybe you should decorate it then for me."

She sliced a hand through the air. "Nonsense!" she exclaimed. "I told you why I leave them as they are."

As she closed the door, I groaned. "I'm not decorating it," I shouted back.

Even if she did catch that, I doubted she'd actually retain it. This woman was as stubborn as a bull. How many times did I have to tell these people I did not like Christmas? I wasn't going to spend my time decorating a freaking tree. Correction: freaking *fake* tree. That was definitely not my idea of a good time.

Not that anyone asked, but my version of fun for the holidays was sitting in the leather chair in my home office with classical music playing in the background and my laptop.

Now that, that right there was a good freaking time.

Just then my phone signaled a new email and I looked down and saw it was from Izzy. *And there we go.* If it wasn't bad enough to be subjected to the Christmas vomit in this room, then quite possibly the most excited person in the world had to be contacting me. Again.

As I opened it, suddenly all I could hear in my head was *fa-la-la-la-la, man, you are in trouble.*

Upon reading it, I realized it actually wasn't so bad. She just wanted to meet up. Big surprise there, especially since she knew I was in town. And it was for Louie and Fiona of course.

How bad could cake tasting be?

I sent back a reply.

From: bo@grantandco.com
To: izzydoesbooks@mymail.com
Subject: Re: In town

Set it up and I'll be there. Wherever there is. I might need a name or address.

Obviously she was sitting around waiting for my reply because I got another notification not two seconds later.

From: izzydoesbooks@mymail.com
To: bo@grantandco.com
Subject: Re: In town

We could call each other if you want to give me your number. Might be easier. Phoebe said in two hours works for her. She'll close early for us. Her bakery's address is below.

Call me? The idea of this woman having my number so she can call me anytime she wanted sent chills down my spine. I didn't even want to think about all of the excited voicemails I'd have from her.

Izzy wasn't bad, by the way. She was nice and considerate, obviously cared a great deal about her friends and loved this town, so all of that had to say something about her. I just wasn't sure what that something was and I still wasn't giving her my number.

From: bo@grantandco.com
To: izzydoesbooks@mymail.com
Subject: Re: In town

Email is good for me. Thanks for the address. See you then.

* * *

Pickleball.

Hiking.

Skiing.

Surfing.

Going to the dentist.

Walking a dog.

All things I'd rather be doing than this.

The this, you ask? Cake tasting.

There are certain things guys should never know. Like the name of their girl's perfume, how much time it takes them to get ready in the morning, where stores are located in the mall, and *anything* having to do with weddings. That included the ins and outs of cake tasting.

You'd think it wasn't complicated to just taste a cake, say you like it and move on. But nope. That wasn't the case. At least it wasn't what was happening here with Izzy.

"Bo," Izzy leaned forward, her face in front of mine, a hand waving in front of me. "Hello, earth to Bo. What do you think of the chocolate raspberry one?"

I shook my head, trying to bring myself back to the here and now. "Hmm?"

"The chocolate raspberry?" she prompted again.

I looked down at the table filled with a variety of cake slices. "It's good," I answered as my eyes ran over each one. Mind you, there were more than a dozen here.

When she didn't respond, only lightly swatting my arm, I asked, "What? I said it was good."

She rolled her eyes. "This is their wedding cake. This is not just some cake. They're going to cut it together, one of their first acts as a newlywed couple. Photos will be taken. They're going to save the top tier for their first anniversary. All of their family and friends will surround them as they take a bite of this cake. I don't think you're understanding just how serious this is." She sighed before continuing to go on, "Sure, the ceremony is important, but the reception is like its baby and the baby needs to be cared for and nurtured. It needs love and attention. It needs a great cake, a kicking seating chart, and a slick dance floor with popping music." Then she narrowed her eyes. "Does that make sense?"

"Yeah, you sort of lost me on the whole baby part." Man, what was she talking about? Izzy needed to come with like a dictionary of her own. Because half the time I swore it was like we spoke two completely different languages.

Not that I ever wanted to learn whatever language she knew, considering half of what she said sounded like mumbo-jumbo to me.

She rolled her eyes and was about to speak when Phoebe brought over yet another platter of cake slices. "Okay," she exclaimed practically breathless, "I have five more options for you. Are there any here we can definitely eliminate?" she asked looking at the table as she made room for the new one.

"Bo likes the chocolate raspberry, but I know Fi and she'd love the lemon."

"Lemon?" I practically gagged. "That was the worst one." Then I looked up at Phoebe and actually felt bad. "No offense," I added.

She smiled and shook her head. "It's not for everyone."

"It tasted like soap," I explained. "And not just yours. Ask anyone and they'll say the same thing," I said, trying to smooth it over.

She shrugged. "I actually like it myself."

"Me, too," Izzy defended.

So that made three, counting Fiona in. "Well, I know Louie," I said, decidedly taking up for my friend, "and he'd want chocolate."

Izzy sighed. "It's not like we can very well have a chocolate lemon cake. Now that sounds disgusting."

Phoebe gave us a lopsided smile. "Can't argue with you there, but what I can do is make an orange chocolate cake."

Izzy brushed her off. "Nah, Fiona gave me explicit instructions: no citrus unless it's lemon."

I harrumphed. "No to orange, but she has no problem with lemon?"

"Would you mind giving us a second, Phoebe?" she asked. "We'll try the new ones and see if we can come to an agreement."

Phoebe started to walk away, but stopped before she hit the back door. "Just so you know, I can always do a groom's cake if they can't agree."

"No," I nixed the idea. "Louie wouldn't want that." I picked up my fork again and reached for some chocolate swirl concoction. It tasted like chocolate, smelled like chocolate. It wasn't bad. "You should try this one."

But Izzy was already shaking her head. "No, no." She shoved her fork in my face. "You have to try this one," she insisted, bringing it to my lips, which I promptly shut and backed up.

Brows furrowed, I studied her. "Are you trying to feed me?"

Laughing, she pushed the fork closer. "Come on, it's fine. Just try this," she said, her hand under the fork. "Bo, open up."

Looking at her, I extended my hand and clutched the fork, trying to remove her hand. "I got this." I slipped it in my mouth and let the flavors do their thing.

Let's just say this: Izzy and I had very different palates. This cake was not good. I swallowed begrudgingly. "What is that?"

"Lavender. Can't you read the tag?"

My eyes went wide. "Lavender?"

"It's sophisticated," she defended.

Shaking my head, I decided I had enough of sitting at this table with her, she who had no tastebuds. I pushed my chair back and stood up. "It's gross. Lavender is for perfume, not consumption."

Sitting back, Izzy heaved a sigh. "I don't know. We can't do this. We're too different."

"No argument there," I said before turning to walk around the otherwise empty bakery. "Listen, it's not about you or me. Louie likes chocolate. He told me he proposed to Fiona with her ring in a piece of chocolate cake, so that means she must like chocolate, too, right?" I asked, trying to wrap this up. "So what's the problem with good old chocolate?"

She shook her head. "That's a good point, but I don't know. There's just so many options. I think we need Phoebe." Then she shouted, "Phoebe! Can you come out here for a minute?"

Pushing open the swinging door from the back, she came out in a hurry. "Did you decide?"

"Not necessarily. We narrowed it to chocolate cake, though. There are just so many," she said, gesturing to the table. "Can you help us?"

Nodding, Phoebe stuck the pencil she had in her hair and adjusted her apron. "Sure." She immediately started removing plates, putting them on the surrounding tables. "These are all the chocolate ones," she pointed to the variety that remained.

I walked over, ready to sit down and pick a cake for crying out loud. "What's this one? I think I liked this," I said, trying to remember. They all looked the same.

"It's got a mocha buttercream filling," Izzy explained, pointing to the card.

Oh, yeah. I picked my fork up and took a bite. "Not bad."

Izzy did the same. "I agree, but I just don't think it's their wedding cake."

"Okay, so we're getting somewhere," Phoebe said optimistically. "Here, try this next. If you liked the mocha, you'll like this."

We each took another bite. I shook my head. "Too sweet."

She removed the plate. "Try this one. It's got cherry."

Izzy scrunched up her face. "Too tart."

She removed the plate and this continued until we were left with one piece. "Well, I think Fiona and Louie have their cake," Phoebe declared triumphantly.

Izzy looked at me, our eyes connecting for the first time all day. "Yeah, I think they do," she agreed.

And that folks, wrapped up the cake tasting portion of the day. "We done here?" I asked, ready to hightail it out of the bakery and find the nearest gym. Although, I had a feeling, I'd have to leave town for that one.

Nodding her head, Izzy signed some papers Phoebe put in front of her. Then Izzy spun around and put her hand up. "Wait!"

"What?"

"You're on my way. Let me drive you back," she declared, a smile creeping across her face as she walked toward me, clutching her purse and digging her keys out.

It was a nice gesture and all, but there was one teeny tiny problem with it. "How do you know where I'm staying?" I hadn't told her. In fact, I'd made sure to never really say. Not that there were many options in this town, but still. I had a fighting chance, didn't I?

Touching my arm, she led us out the door. "I don't."

"So how can you be sure it's on your way?" I asked, eyebrow raised.

She threw her head back in laughter. "Everything's on my way. You remember I own the bookstore, right? Well, that's at the back of town, right before you hit Lakespur. I almost didn't buy the place because it was so out of the way."

Staring at her hand clutching my arm, I wondered when she'd let go. "And yet you did."

She nodded. "I did," she responded, oblivious to the fact that she was still touching me and I didn't know why.

In New York I knew this kind of thing could get a person arrested for battery, but here apparently it was no big deal to just touch strangers. It was interesting and much too friendly for me.

"So where are you staying?" she tried again.

Groaning, I knew I didn't stand a chance. Sooner or later someone would see me. Or Holly herself would go blabbering. So I swallowed hard and tugged my arm free of her grasp. "Holly's B&B."

Her face lit up like one of those Christmas lights I'm sure Izzy loved as she unlocked her car door. "Perfect. Get in."

This was anything but perfect, but who was I to argue with her? We'd done enough of that at the bakery, going a few rounds over cake.

I opened the passenger door and slid in.

"So which room are you in?" she asked as she started the car and pulled away from the curb. "Holly decorates all the rooms in themes this time of year. Isn't that just adorable?"

"Precious."

"Well, which did you get? I have a particular fondness for the room dedicated to Scrooge."

My eyebrow shot up at that one and I turned to eye this woman who just said the most contradictory thing I'd ever heard.

"What?" she asked, taking her eyes off the road and looking at me when I didn't respond right away.

I shook my head. "It's nothing. I'm just surprised, is all. You, liking Scrooge." In fact, it went against everything I knew about Izzy Monroe. Wasn't this the same woman who took a stand for candy canes?

Laughing, she diverted her gaze back to the road. "I didn't say I liked Scrooge. I just like the way she does the room. She blends past, present and future nicely. She also has those old timey clothes hanging as decor, it's just perfectly done. That's all I was saying. So what's your deal? You hate Christmas or something?"

Did I hate Christmas? Yes, I did. But was I about to confess that to *her*? No. Certainly not with her behind the wheel. I valued my life way too much, thank you very much. "No. It's just. . . not my favorite holiday." And that was counting in days like Flag Day, Martin Luther King's Birthday, Washington's Birthday, oh and you couldn't forget about Columbus Day.

Then to my great surprise, Izzy challenged me. "You're lying. You hate Christmas, don't you? You hate the happiest day of the year? I bet you also hate all this wedding stuff. And hugs, tiny babies, and butterflies, don't you?"

Reeling from the list and the way she just nailed me, I angled my head and pulled back, the seatbelt suddenly feeling like it was choking me. "No," was all I could manage to croak out.

Her eyes going wide, she looked back at me again. "It's true. Who hurt you Bo?" she asked, sadness in her eyes.

I shook my head. "I'm not having this conversation with you. I like those things just fine. I do have a life, though, and they just aren't a very big part of it. Big deal. I even have a small Christmas tree in my room, I'll have you know. Holly delivered it this morning."

Laughing again, she waved a hand in the air. "So what? I bet you don't plan on decorating it. You probably already calculated it to see how much fire wood you can make out of it."

"It's fake," I pointed out. She didn't know me as well as she thought she did.

"Whatever," she said. Then she turned in front of the B&B and came to a stop. "You should decorate it, you know. It's Christmas destiny."

"It's Christmas destiny?" This sounded oddly like Holly's whole "the tree looks sad" theory.

She nodded. "Sure. Trees like that are meant to be decorated. Just like the big one in the center of town square."

Yeah, the big, gargantuan tree that could easily be on television. I'd seen it. I'd also heard about the tree decorating thing. "Maybe you should spearhead decorating that and leave me and my small, fake tree alone." My hand was on the door handle, ready to make my escape once and for all, but her next words stopped me.

"We already do that. It's an annual tradition. One night in December the whole town comes out and we decorate the tree. We use the balls with our names on them. A gift from our city chairman for all residents once we call Silver Springs home. They're rather lovely, hand-painted by one of our own, I'll have you know, because I can already see the wrinkles forming on your forehead like you're confused or disgusted," she said, pointing to the space between my eyes. "It's about being part of a community."

Trying to smooth out my forehead, I nodded. "Sounds nice. Well, this is me," I stated the obvious and opened the door, not sure I was made for this whole community thing she talked about.

Chapter Six

Izzy

"I'm telling you, it should be a requirement that on first dates you both wear a name tag with your full names, especially when it's essentially a blind date." I listened to Zel, one of my very best friends, as she regaled me with the details of her first date with this guy she met on a dating app. The only thing was, this dating app didn't have photos on the profiles because they claimed it distracted from what was really important—the inside, a person's heart and personality.

Zel was every man's fantasy—long, blonde hair, green eyes, well-endowed, and knew how to have a good time— and yet, she was still single. Her mother wouldn't let her date when she was in high school, swearing that boys only wanted one thing. I didn't think I needed to spell out what that one thing was, we all knew what she was talking about. But men, well, were they really any different? Although, Zel blamed that for the reason she was still single, said she could've been with her high school sweetheart now. If she had one.

To me, the chances seemed slim, but I wasn't going to burst her bubble.

Zel pulled open the door to the clothing store and I fixed my shopping bags on my arm as we walked in. "So let me get this straight," I said, trying to make sense of the disaster that was Zel's date last night. "You were supposed to be on a date with, er, John, but instead you were having dinner with some other guy who was supposed to be on a blind date of his own—we'll call him Not John—who you did not swipe right on?"

Zel nodded and then chuckled. "Hey, I think I like that. John and Not John. Cute. Anyway, what are the odds they were both named John; crazy, right?" As we started walking through the store, her eyes landed on a rack full of fleece-lined leggings. "You can never have too many warm leggings, right? And these are nice. I don't have tan ones." Pulling at the fabric, she eyed me. "What do you think? Should I try them on?"

"Definitely." Steering the conversation back to the date, I asked, "So then what happened? You know, after Real John showed up."

Taking the hanger off the rack, she blew bubbles and gripped the bridge of her nose with her free hand. "I was so done, sick of the whole thing that I called it a night. I mean, and the real kicker is that Real John was so handsome. Nothing like Not John who sat across the table from me and picked spinach out of his teeth while we waited for dessert."

"Yikes." I let out an exasperated noise. "I'm surprised you stuck around for dessert. Not John sounds horrible."

She rolled her eyes. "I know," she agreed. "But dessert is the best part, right? And he started crying when I brought up bringing out the check. He said it was bringing back vivid memories of the time he was rejected by the cheer captain, which was making him want to cry and then he actually did. Cry, I mean."

I cringed. "You have the worst luck with dates, but this one might just be the worst yet. Honestly, it sounds like you should've been the one crying."

"You're telling me. I can't believe I drove all the way into Asheville for it. Whoever I saved him from was one lucky lady."

"Yeah, or she thought she was stood up and went home and cried about it."

Laughing, she shook her head. "Whatever. I'm thinking they should use my date as an example for the definition of the word 'waste' in the dictionary."

I couldn't help but laugh. "Stop," I replied.

"Real John and I agreed to try it again. We have a date set for next weekend and, at least this time, I know who I'm meeting." Shaking her shoulders, as though trying to rid herself of the thoughts and icky experiences, she changed the topic. "You know, I'm really excited for Fiona's wedding."

"Fiona's wedding," I repeated. "Don't even get me started on that. I'm working with quite literally the grumpiest man ever." I shot her a look as we continued browsing. "Bo hates Christmas."

She gasped, her head whipping around to look at me. "How can that be?" Then she started laughing. "I'm sorry. I just couldn't help myself."

I pursed my lips and gave her a look as though to say, "Are you done?"

"It's just, not everyone loves the holidays as much as you. Are you sure he hates Christmas? Maybe he just doesn't want to wear jingle bell socks and, I don't know, knit stockings."

I rolled my eyes. Okay, so I saw her point. I was slightly more obsessed with Christmas than most, but since when was that a bad thing? "No, he seems to have an aversion to it. He says he doesn't hate it, but I don't think that's true. And planning this wedding with his help is torture. He doesn't get the whole wedding thing, either."

"Well, I say you invite him to Jesse and Nancy's ugly sweater party." Wagging her eyes, she pushed, "Come on! It could be so much fun and now that I know this about him, seeing him in a pool of all those sweaters might just be the highlight of my year."

"Seems cruel." Then I added, "For the other people who have to hear his snarls."

She waved me off. "We can get him one. I happen to need to shop for a new one anyway. I'm certainly not wearing the same one as last year."

I licked my lips and thought about what she said. Bo aside, I could've burst out laughing at the mere thought of last year's sweater. Let's just say it moved—and not because it was on Zel, but actually moved on its own—and lit up. Zel insisted we burned the photos, but Nancy framed one since she was the winner at the party.

It was an annual thing and the person who showed up with the ugliest one won the contest. You didn't really win anything other than bragging rights, but it was still fun. Not that I would ever win because while I chose cheesy sweaters, I never selected anything quite as bad as the one Zel did. Even Holly gave us all a good run for our money. I didn't know where she shopped, but every year, she seemed to have a more over-the-top sweater. It'd been a couple of years since she won, but I had a feeling she was going to try to steal back the title this year.

"Deal. Nothing too gaudy."

Holding up the leggings, she decided, "I'm not going to try these on," walking over to the counter to be rung up. "I'm just going to buy them."

I nodded and walked with her. "So how's the painting going for Fiona and Louie?" I asked as she was rung up.

She smiled and gushed, "Amazing. Seriously, I cannot believe you did this for them. They're going to love it. I would want someone to get me a wedding gift like that one day."

It wasn't that big of a deal. I commissioned a painting from a photograph of when he proposed and planned on giving it to them as a wedding present. Zel was one of the most talented artists I knew, so it was a no-brainer.

"Do you ever think about when it'll be your turn?" Zel asked somewhat out of the blue. Although, I knew exactly what she was talking about.

"Too often," I answered earnestly. "I want someone who's excited about the things I am, who shares in my achievements, and makes it their mission to put a smile on my face." I shrugged as she grabbed the bag and we turned to leave. "It's silly, really."

"No, it's not silly at all. One day you'll get that. But don't be surprised if he doesn't check all the boxes. Love is unexpected."

Chapter Seven

Bo

I was right. This gingerbread latte was way too sweet and I immediately regretted ordering the thing. I was in line for a coffee, though, and saw every patron leaving with one, so I gave in and figured I'd give it a try. What a mistake.

Just like I thought, I mused, as I swallowed another gulp and held the cup out to eye it—I needed to make a dentist appointment as soon as possible. Maybe even a doctor's appointment so they could take my blood to test my levels. You know, the cholesterol in that thing alone could give me a heart attack.

I sat at the desk in my room and put the drink down. I didn't even finish a quarter of it and already my stomach was sick. See, that was what happened when I listened to these people and their ramblings about how black coffee was too bitter. Well, one person in particular. . . Izzy.

I raked a hand through my hair and touched the small tree Holly left with me. It did look rather festive with the snow it was sitting on. No, no, no.

What was I thinking?

Fake snow.

Fake tree.

Fake holiday bologna.

Shaking my head, I went to check my email when there was a knock on the door. I really hoped it wasn't Holly trying to convince me to go caroling with the rest of them tonight. She brought it up a few times already and my answer was a hard no. Nothing changed since then. Well, except that I bought a gingerbread latte, but other than that, nothing was different.

It was nearly instinct to close the door as soon as I saw who was on the other side. "Izzy." My eyes scanned her brown hair that was free-flowing in loose waves over her shoulders, her lips that looked perfectly pink. . . okay, officially backing it up now and focusing on anything besides her lips. Oh, look, she was wearing white fuzzy boots. But noticing those only made me realize how great her legs looked, and before I knew it I was taking in her red dress, too, and how it hugged her curves. Geez, what was I doing?

"Before you go freaking out, let me explain." Izzy's voice interrupted my thoughts and had my eyes immediately darting back to hers.

I swallowed hard and pulled at the back of my neck. "What are you talking about? Why would I freak out?"

That was when she raised her arms up and I noticed the bags she was carrying in her hands. "The bags," she said, tilting her head and quirking a brow. "These are what had your eyes getting all wide, right?"

Hmm, sure, let's go with that. Because the truth had me coming off as a creeper. Worse, an ogling creeper. I lightly laughed. "You caught me. Those bags have me quaking over here." Then I cleared my throat. "So what's in them?"

Clearly ignoring my question, she decided to ask her own, "May I come in?" She peered behind me into the room now. "I hope you don't mind, by the way, but Holly told me where I could find you. In all our talk the other day about the Scrooge room, you never did tell me which one you got."

I opened the door more and stepped to the side. "No problem."

I watched as she looked around the room, her head angling. "This room is beautiful, isn't it? There's just something about snow globes that are so—" she paused, clearly searching for the right word.

I tried helping, offering up, "Magical."

Obviously surprised by my opinion that they were magical, she turned and studied me. "Yes, that was exactly what I was thinking."

I shrugged. "They're pretty. I used to like shaking them when I was a kid, watching the snow fall. It made me feel like there was a sliver of joy to be found in a somewhat dim world."

She frowned and I shook my head, trying to avoid the awkward apology that my upbringing wasn't all sugar cones and candy canes. "Anyway, what are you here for again?"

Shutting the door, I walked up beside her and watched as she placed the bags on the chair at the desk and sighed, turning around. "I came bearing gifts."

"Better watch out," I warned, "you might make Santa angry for stealing his job. Doesn't he deliver the presents?"

"Cute," she said and for the first time I heard something she said drip with sarcasm. "Call it what you will. Christmas coming early, whatever, but these are for you."

"It's nice you went shopping for me, but you didn't have to."

She narrowed her eyes. "Oh, Bo, if ever there was a shopping emergency, this was it."

Okay, now I was slightly scared. What was in those bags? Before I could get a word in or consider all the possibilities, she whipped out something from one of the bags.

"Ta-da!" she exclaimed, holding up a sweater of some sort against her body. "What do you think?"

I cocked a brow. "Looks a little big for you."

"It's not for me, silly. This is for you," she said, shoving it at me.

I backed up, though, my hands in the air, not wanting to touch it. I shook my head. "Uh, uh, no way." I imagined my eyes were practically bugging out of my head at this point. "You said this was a shopping emergency, but I don't remember asking for this, this. . . thing. It's the ugliest thing I've ever seen in my life." It was green with garland and silver and gold bells hanging off of it. Are you getting the picture? Ugly was the only way to describe it. In fact, remember the reindeer one Holly wore where it was practically coming out of the sweater? This one might've been worse. No, scratch that, it was one-hundred percent worse.

She shook her head and tried to pawn it off on me again. "It being ugly is sort of the whole point."

"The point in what?" *Scaring young children?*

"So glad you asked."

That made one of us. "Actually, forget I asked. I don't want to know. It's a nice gesture, but no thank you."

She tossed it on the bed and came closer. "Every year, Jesse—" Then she paused. "You remember Jesse, right?"

I nodded.

"Well, every year he and his wife Nancy host an ugly Christmas sweater party. It's the most hopping party of the year and most everyone in town attends."

Under my breath, 1 mumbled, "Why am I not surprised?"

She pursed her lips and crossed her arms. "There's a contest and whoever wears the ugliest sweater wins. It's actually quite fun and there's ga—"

I held up a hand. "Let me stop you right there. Based on the fact that you bought me a sweater and are telling me all of this, I'm going to go out on a limb here and assume you think I'm attending."

She nodded and tapped her nose. "Bingo! I happen to know you're going because you're coming with me."

Two words: no way. I shook my head so she'd get the picture. "I don't think so."

She let out an exasperated sigh. "Do you really want to go back and forth on this all day long? Or do you want to see what's in the bags?" She reached over the chair and started pulling more stuff out.

I scratched my chin and looked over her shoulder as she pulled out packages. Laying them on the table, I took in each one.

Garland.

Lights that didn't light, so they were fake?

Ornaments.

And more ornaments.

"Is this for my tree?"

She nodded. "Bingo again! You're good at this," she patronized me and rolled her eyes. It was the first bit of sass I saw from her and I had to say, I didn't hate it. Maybe I was rubbing off on her. I shook away the thought as she continued, "Come on, it'll be fun. It's the tree's destiny, remember?"

I backed up, trying to get away from all the Christmas she was tossing out on what was formerly serving as my desk. This felt like the ultimate violation of my space, but would Izzy understand that? I thought not. "Fine, I have a feeling I don't get a say in this, so let's decorate." Then she'd leave and I could get on with my life, I thought to myself.

"That's the spirit," Izzy said, completely missing my tone and the underlying sentiment.

I reached for the tree and decided we could do this on the table, but she stopped me. "No. Leave it where you want it, so we don't have to move it. It seems like where it is sitting on the snow is perfect." She walked over and patted the snow around it and smiled. "Yeah, let's do it here."

"Whatever you say." I walked back to the table and examined all the stuff she collected for the world's smallest tree. "Will all this stuff fit on it? It seems like a lot."

"Have you never decorated a tree before?" she asked, her eyebrows in the air as she waited for me to answer.

I shrugged. "I'm sure when I was little. We did a lot of stuff like this until my grandmother died."

"How old were you?"

"Six. Maybe seven, I think."

She whistled as she walked over and started sorting through the things, opening packages as she went. "That was a long time ago. Well, that's okay, I'm here now and I can walk you through it. First, the lights go up."

"They're fake." I couldn't help myself, I had to say it as I tapped the plastic, painted bulbs.

She laughed. "It's the suggestion of lights. Here, I'll show you." She walked to the tree and started at the top, draping the strand all around it in a circular motion until she reached the bottom. "We want them to sit on the branches, not necessarily get buried and not sit on the edge, either. Now we will layer the garland in the same way, but with garland, you want it to sit on the edges a bit more, don't shove it in. It's about a gentle touch." Seemingly satisfied with the lesson she gave me, she passed me the garland.

I looked down at it and wondered if I'd get it right. No time like the present to try, and the sooner I played along, the sooner I could have my room back to myself. I walked over to the tree and mimicked her motions from before. "Like this?"

She approached and nodded. "Exactly."

As I got to the bottom, she reached over and laid her hand on mine. "Like this when you come to the bottom," she said as she guided my hand.

When we finished, she stepped back and looked at me. "Good job for a first timer."

I nodded. "Now what?"

She walked back to the table and retrieved the ornaments.

"What about the star?" I'd seen it on the table. You couldn't miss it really. It was the biggest, shiniest silver, glitter-covered thing in the mix.

"You could do it now or at the end. On a real tree I usually do it now to not drop the ornaments as I reach up there, but this guy's so small, I think you can do it whenever you want."

I reached for it. "I think I'd like to do it now." I held it in my hands and studied it. This might have been the first time I really looked at a tree topper. It was nice.

I slipped it on and backed up. "It looks good." I looked over at her and put my hands together. "What do you think?"

Her eyes met mine immediately and she grinned, her cheeks turning a soft blush. "I think," she started in a voice lower than normal. Without looking back at the tree, still intent on my eyes, she said, "It looks beautiful."

Clearing my throat, I clapped my hands together now to break the trance and whatever the heck was going on. "Great. Do you think the ornaments will clutter it?"

She shook her head. "No. It needs ornaments to finish the look. On my tree, I have lots of handmade ones from when I was younger. Even my father made a few, carving them out of wood. He was always inventing one thing or another when I was growing up, so working with his hands was so natural to him."

As I listened to her talk about her father and her childhood, I felt something in my gut I wasn't used to feeling. I didn't know what it was. Sadness probably. Sadness for the fact that those were moments and memories I didn't have. My parents were not the nurturing type, especially my father, who was all business, all the time.

Pulling me from my rogue thoughts, Izzy hung an ornament and stopped, asking me, "What's the story behind the ring you wear?"

I looked down at the black band on my finger and cleared my throat. "What makes you think there's a story?"

She angled her head. "It's not a wedding ring and yet you always wear it. Just figured. Am I wrong?"

I touched it, spinning it around my finger before taking it off and studying the one thing I never took off. "It was my grandfather's. When I was a boy, my grandmother gave it to me. She told me how she saved it for me. We shared the same name and it's an initial ring, so," I let my words trail off as I considered how much more I should say.

"His name was Bo?"

"Actually, it's Beauregard," I answered, then thought better of this conversation. "Geez, what's with the third degree? Trying to collect information so you can sell it to some blog as soon as I'm out of here?" It wouldn't have been the first time a woman betrayed me.

She frowned and lowered her voice, saying, "I wouldn't do that."

I watched her closely, my eyes searching hers. I wasn't sure what I was looking for, but I was definitely looking. Maybe for the truth. Maybe for the darkness, the bad. Everyone had some piece of that in them, didn't they? My jaw ticked when I couldn't find anything.

"May I say something?" Izzy asked suddenly.

"You might as well. It doesn't seem like you resist speaking your mind often, do you?"

"Speak my mind, yes, but hurt someone, no. I'd never set out to hurt another person, even someone like you."

My voice roared as I asked, "What does that mean?"

"I try, Bo. I really do. I like to think I'm a pleasant person, but around you, I have to work so much harder at it, trying harder to be happy just to overcompensate for your. . . your—"

"What?" I'd love to hear this.

"Bad moods! I don't know how you can be so unpleasant all the time. It must be lonely being you, not trusting people, not knowing kindness. Frankly, I feel sorry for you," she said and spun on her heel, almost like she was thinking about leaving.

Well, I wouldn't stop her.

But then she turned to face me again and I could see how much this affected her, how hard she was trying. She looked almost sad. So I did the one thing I said I wouldn't do—stop her. "Wait. Let's try this again. After all, we have to finish decorating my tree, right?" I questioned, hoping that was enough to keep her here.

She nodded and walked closer to me again. "Izzy Rose Monroe," she said simply, but then added, "that's my name. Rose was my aunt's name."

"Izzy Rose Monroe," I repeated. "I like that. Thank you for sharing that with me."

She shrugged casually as she started added more ornaments to the tree. "Felt only right since you shared. I like Beauregard, by the way, it's a nice, strong name. It suits you."

I nodded and kept adding the ornaments that had to be no bigger than an inch or two to the tree. It was really coming together. Who would've guessed how nice it was having a tree you decorated? "How many more should we add?" I asked, looking at the haul she got and examining the tree. There was barely any space left.

"Lots," she said, laughter in her voice. "All of them. We want it to look full and festive. I even got miniature candy canes that we can hang off the branches sporadically. I know how much you love candy canes." Izzy winked at me and I laughed, remembering the day I came back to town and we ran into to each other at the coffee shop.

"Funny."

She walked back to her bags and started digging through them. "They're here somewhere. I went shopping with my friend and we might have overdone it."

"I'll say. That's a lot of bags."

She shook her head. "This isn't even the half of it. I left most of them in my car. Clothes, gifts, the works."

"The banks must love you," I said, imagining her credit card bills.

"If I overindulge once a year, I'm okay with that. I love giving gifts. There's something about seeing the way a person's face lights up when you show them you thought about them. It's like magic."

I wasn't sure what to say. I didn't really know what she was talking about. Aside from Mirna, who I wrote a big, fat check for every year, I didn't really give anyone gifts. There was no one in my life who I wanted to do that for, I guessed. Louie was my best friend, but he was a dude and we just didn't swap gifts. Take trips to golf or take in a game every once in a while, sure, but exchange gifts? We never did it. Finally, I confessed. "I'll have to take your word for it."

Izzy's eyes connected with mine and she smiled. It started out small, but then grew, touching her eyes. I only wished I knew what she was thinking, but I shook it off, decidedly seeing the good in her, in anyone, for the first time in a long time.

"Can I ask you something?" she ventured, seemingly hesitant, likely from my overreaction before, but I was really trying here, so I nodded. "Why do you hate Christmas?"

Not sure that was a road I wanted to go down, I stuck with the same story I gave her before. "I don't hate Christmas."

That was when she threw leftover garland at me. "You so do! Don't deny it. It's so obvious. What is it about the holiday?"

Playing with the garland I caught, I started wrapping it around my hand. "I don't know. What is it about the holiday that has everyone acting so fake all the time? It just feels so forced." I thought back to all the smiling faces I saw when I first entered town this time around. It was ludicrous.

Waving a candy cane in the air, she laughed. "Why do you assume it's forced? Can't people just be happy? The weather's nice. Decorations are quite literally everywhere you turn. How can a person not be happy?"

Giving up, I tossed the garland back at her. "Not everyone sees the good in everything. If you break it down, it's just another day."

"Nah," she said, wrapping the garland around her like a boa. "Anyway, it's okay because we're going to fix this."

"What?" I lifted a few candy canes from the box and started hanging them off the garland on her, not even thinking about our conversation, just enjoying the moment.

"You hating Christmas," she reminded me, her head at an angle as she studied me.

Oh, yeah, that. As much as I thought she wanted to, she just wasn't getting it, that much was obvious. "No, really, it's nothing that can be fixed. I just don't like Christmas. It's not a big deal. Plus, it seems like something I'd have to work out on my own." *Not that I would.* I stuffed my hands in my pockets and backed up, bringing my attention back to the tree. The whole reason she was here in the first place.

"You don't. I want to help turn this around for you. Let me help," she insisted.

"Let's just finish my tree."

She waved me off. "Forget what I said about covering it, it looks great!"

Sighing, I suddenly wanted to get as far from my room and Izzy as possible. "Is there anything I can say that will have you changing your mind?"

"Nope."

"Then it seems like I'm in for a real treat."

"Oh, you don't know the half of it and we're starting with the ugly sweater party. You're coming," she insisted, picking the garland up again and dancing it in front of her, as if she could entice me with that thing.

But I also knew when to give in, so I did. "Fine. I'll go to the party."

"You're not going to regret it," she said and ran up to me, enveloping me in a hug, which by the way was something else I rarely engaged in. Hugs just weren't my thing, so it felt only natural that I so desperately wanted to escape it.

Chapter Eight

Izzy

It **had been fifteen** minutes since Fiona arrived at my house. Now that the trial had ended and they settled at the eleventh hour, she was as free as a bird, which was clearly a very good thing considering the way she was acting like she'd been cooped up in a barn for years with no one to talk to but the horses.

Fiona flopped backward on the couch, grabbed a pillow nearby, brought it to her chest and closed her eyes as she let out a happy sigh. "This feels so good. I've missed this."

I chuckled as I floated a couple marshmallows in our hot cocoas.

Her eyes, now opened, went as wide as the rim of the mug as she tossed the pillow aside and leaned forward. "Are those the extra large marshies?" She nearly choked, grabbing her chest with her hand.

I cocked my head to the side, extending my arm and passing her a mug. "Please, is that even a question? All other marshmallows are inferior."

Her eyes practically sparkled as her lips touched the mug and she sipped. "Okay, I'm done with being ridiculous."

I nodded and took a sip of mine before snapping my fingers. It needed a touch of peppermint extract.

"Wait!" she exclaimed, putting her mug on the coffee table, getting off the couch and following me into the kitchen. She placed her hands on my shoulders and looked into my eyes. "It's just. . . I've been away for so long, stuck in the trial that I swore would never end." She sighed. "I was beginning to forget what all my favorite people look like. Ugh, I was gone for so long and no time to flip through photos on my phone to remind me. You were becoming a green blob of goo in my mind."

I furrowed my brows. "A green goo blob?"

She tossed her hands up and clapped her thighs when they came back down. "Beats me. And on late nights when I was studying case files, looking through evidence, and strategizing questions for witnesses and every establishment was closed, I was so hungry I thought I could actually bite my own arm off. In fact, there were times I'd think about Louie and see a giant pancake."

"You see Louie as a giant pancake?"

She nodded and side stepped so I could get to the refrigerator for that extract. Don't get me wrong, hot cocoa was great, but peppermint hot cocoa was ten times better. As I opened the fridge, grabbed the extract, and put a bit in my drink, I looked up to see her holding a spoon for me to stir it.

She went on, "I just don't know what to do with myself now that I'm free. It's sort of weird, actually. I'm so used to being consumed with work and that trial." She shuddered. "The thought of going to, say, a movie or something is like mind-boggling to me."

I grinned. "Maybe you need a night out on the town." I took a sip again and sighed in contentment. "Peppermint?" I asked before returning it to the fridge.

She shook her head.

"You must be glad Louie will be done traveling soon."

"Yeah, but it's not like I sit around waiting for him."

I arched a brow. "Where'd that come from? I didn't say that."

"I don't know. Sorry." She fussed with her hair, tucking some loose strands behind her ears before tossing her head back, grunting, and heading back to the couch. "I think I just need to see him again, you know? To remind me why I'm getting married in the first place."

I followed her to the couch where I put my mug on the coffee table beside hers and sat down, tucking my feet under me. I faced her and tried to get a read on her, but came up short. "Okay, what's going on? This doesn't sound like you at all. You and Louie have always been meant to be."

She looked up and shook her head. "I don't know. I mean, what makes us so meant to be? Is it because we love the same things? Because there's plenty we disagree on." Then she leaned in and practically whispered, "And hearing about his job actually bores me, like could put me to sleep bored."

I smacked my lips together. "Fi, most everyones' jobs are boring. That doesn't mean you two don't belong together."

Leaning her head back, she groaned. "Fifty percent of marriages end in divorce. We'd have better luck forgetting the stupid piece of paper and just staying together like we are—engaged, living together. It would be so much easier that way, right? So if it doesn't work out we can easily go our separate ways without getting anyone involved or making things complicated. And, oof, what if there are kids involved when we decide to separate?"

"All right, you listen to me." I grew serious and spoke with my hands. "You make it sound so certain, but it's not. There's a big if there and more."

She shrugged. "It could happen."

"There are a million reasons why two people should never get together, should never even commit to one another so that they don't have to worry about the future that's so unclear. But throwing in the towel is not the answer. You and Louie have always wanted to be together. And sometimes the heart wants what it wants and we have no choice but to listen to it. Honestly, if you ask me, the scariest thing is when we don't listen to it."

My mind began reeling and for some reason I kept thinking about Bo, how even though I didn't want to admit it, a piece of me was so curious about him, about what it would be like to be with a man like him. Maybe we weren't compatible on paper, but sometimes these things—like who we were attracted to—couldn't be helped.

She quirked a brow and gave me a questioning look that had my stomach clenching. "Are we still talking about Louie and I?"

Was I that obvious?

"Of course," I answered far too quickly. "Who else would I be talking about?" *Feigning ignorance, that was the way to go here.*

Shrugging, she answered, "Oh, I don't know, perhaps you and Bo. I happen to know firsthand how much time you two have been spending together lately."

I brushed her off. "That's ridiculous and only because of you, might I remind you. There is nothing between Bo and I."

But what if I wanted there to be?

I shook my head at that thought.

No, absolutely not.

What was I thinking?

Even one date with that man would be a recipe for disaster.

"Please," I went on, with a little too much protest, even to my own ears. "You've been with your head in those legal documents or whatever for way too long." I got up and began spiraling. "Bo and I are too different. Plus, he doesn't even see me as anything more than your maid of honor and probably a nuisance." I stammered, sort of nervous I couldn't come up with enough reasons why we weren't good for one another. *Ha, got it!* "I made him decorate a tree even though he doesn't like Christmas."

"The horror!" One of her hands flew to her mouth and she gasped.

Obviously, she was mocking me, so I gave her my best bite-me look and crossed my arms.

"Make sure he doesn't go to the police with that information because you might end up in a holding cell. I mean, that has to be some sort of crime, right?" She smiled. "I'm sorry, Izzy. It's just, she who doth protest too much," she let her words trail off. "Besides, I always saw potential there."

"It's because you're all googly eyes for Louie, you can't see straight," I tried more casually, but I knew she was right. Heck, I thought the same thing before the words even came flying out of my mouth, but what else was I supposed to do? It wasn't like I could admit that I thought Bo was cute—okay, criminally handsome.

And that day that I stopped by with shopping bags and we decorated his tree, don't think I didn't notice how adorable he was hanging that garland or those little candy canes off me. Was it possible he was opening himself up to the joy of the season? Or at least me?

Maybe I was delusional.

But then why would he talk a little about his past and his given name?

I was getting confused. I was just trying to help the man like Christmas while he was here, enjoy himself a little, you know? That was all. And plan the wedding. But thankfully that was all just about done now.

Yeah, Fiona was misreading the whole thing. "Subject change, please," I insisted finally, getting out of my own head long enough to say that.

She kicked her feet in the air and chuckled. "You are so obvious. How is it that Bo can't see it when he's around you? Because there's no way you hide it any better around him."

I rolled my eyes and fussed with my fingers, playing with my cuticles. "You're one of my best friends," I mumbled noncommittally.

She shot up like a jack in the box and pointed a finger at me. "Ah-ha! So you admit it? You're feeling some sort of way about Bo."

I grabbed her finger and pushed it away from my general direction. "Yeah, sympathy. I feel bad for him and the way he grew up. Any man who can grow up to be as grumpy as he is must've had a difficult upbringing. Plus, it seems like he's been burned in the past, maybe by an ex-girlfriend, because he has deep-seated trust issues." *Hello, he thought I'd sell his personal information to a blog! I would never do something like that.*

Wagging her eyebrows up and down, she playfully goaded me, "You like him."

I reached over and grabbed my hot cocoa, missing the marshmallows that so obviously melted. "I'm not looking for a heartbreaker, okay? Someone that's just going to be here one day, making me feel some sort of way about him"— I put that last part in air quotes—"only to be caught off guard and left feeling empty when he leaves." Which he would, I knew. Leave, that was.

Bo had no intention of staying.

And so what if I was starting to look at him differently?

That changed nothing, right?

We had no future, so what was the point in having a present?

Chapter Nine

Bo

I **tugged at the** neck of my sweater. "I can't believe I'm wearing this in public." Or at all. What was Izzy thinking when she bought this thing? Better yet, what was I thinking when I put it on?

"Come on, it's not that bad."

I looked down again for good measure. Yeah, yeah, it was. "On the contrary. Mine *is* that bad. You clearly had it out for me when you picked this up for me. I jingle as I walk, Izzy. I feel like a cat with all of these bells."

She laughed. She actually laughed at me. Could you believe the nerve of her? I eyed her, my eyes thin slits as I waited for her to say something.

"They didn't have a lot of options. Plus, it's an ugly Christmas sweater party, everyone wears something tacky, it's kind of the whole point. You're worrying about this too much." She took a step and then turned back to wait for me.

Meanwhile, I took in her red and green sweater with a gold, three-dimensional bow on her chest. "Even you're wearing a less ridiculous sweater," I said, trying to get her to see reason.

"Oh, please," she started, "it's fine and we look sillier just standing outside. Let's go in. Look, the Martins just arrived." Her eyes were drawn just beyond me.

I turned to get a load of the couple, not that I knew who the Martins were. He was wearing one strung with Christmas lights. Ones that actually lit up, not fake ones like on my tree. I pitied the guy on the arm of his wife, smiling at us as he passed us by on the walkway.

"See, that thing lit up," Izzy said, her voice low. "Yours could've been much worse, Bo."

"Yeah, well, any worse and I definitely wasn't wearing it."

"Can we go in now?"

"Fine, but I'm not playing any ridiculous games, so just forget about it right now," I warned her and tugged at the neck of my sweater again, looking around. With all the cars outside, I knew it would be a packed house. That meant it'd be warm and this sweater was already suffocating me.

"Who said you had to?" she asked coyly.

I raised an eyebrow. I doubted she wasn't expecting me to play games. As we stepped inside, I surveyed the full house.

Meanwhile, she obviously wasn't done teasing me, because she pointed out, "Now, they have boxes and bows, wreaths and even a roast beef, so try not to steal any of it."

I turned to look at her, not sharing in her amusement. "Because I'm a grinch, I get it. Ha, ha," I said in mock laughter. "You know, you should do stand-up."

Pleased with herself, she raised her shoulders and tilted her head, smiling so intensely that her cheeks looked like those of a chipmunk. "Thank you."

Turning my attention from her, I looked around again. Izzy was right, the whole town practically turned up for this party. Being an outsider myself, I didn't recognize anyone, so when the man with the lit up sweater stood nearby holding a drink, I stepped over to him.

"Mr. Martin, is it?" I asked, leaning forward. When he nodded, I introduced myself. "Bo Grant."

He smiled. "I know who you are. It's a small town, remember," he said, amusement in his voice.

Small town, that was right. I nodded. "I have to ask. Is it remote controlled?"

Laughing, he nodded and slipped the handheld remote from the pocket of his pants. "Yeah, isn't it great?"

"Great," I repeated, smiling and nodding, figuring I might as well speak their language. What was that saying— when in Rome?

* * *

Izzy

Look at him. Look at the way he just walked away and started talking to Mr. Martin and then several others. It was nothing short of a miracle.

Not that he couldn't pick up a conversation with strangers, but that he wanted to.

At this Christmas party.

With people who were definitely not his kind of people.

Now before you go getting your feathers up, I could say that because I was one of these people—small town folk. At least that was what we were to people like Bo, those from the Big Apple and all that. Not that we walked around with straw in our teeth, but to us community mattered, neighbors, friendships, and Bo had made it plenty clear that those weren't his things. He just didn't get it.

So to see him now, sitting with several of Jesse's friends in the living room, drinking a glass of eggnog. . . I could hardly believe it!

Belle came over and bumped my shoulder, breaking me from my reverie. "Why do you keep staring at that handsome man? Go over and talk to him," she encouraged.

Naturally, she made me smile. Belle was one of the sweetest, if not sassiest people I knew, but she really wasn't one to stay up-to-date on town gossip. She worked herself, running an antique shop where she stocked and repaired old treasures, so if it didn't come through her shop, she simply had no idea about it—Bo included, it seemed. "That's Bo. He came with me, actually. He's Louie's best man from New York," I explained.

She nodded, her blonde bun going up and down with her head. "Oh, that's right! So that's Bo, huh? He's cute. I like the beard, makes him look gruff. If you came together why aren't you with him?" she asked, her head angled as she studied me. "Clearly you want to be over there with him. It's written all over your face."

What was it with everyone? "It's not. I was just thinking how the big city guy could actually mesh with our small town."

She hummed, taking a sip of her drink. "Mmhmm. Maybe those thoughts are really more about how you wished he'd stay and that's why you care whether he meshes well."

"Stop," I insisted. "That's not what this is." And my face better get on board if it kept giving off the wrong kind of looks.

"If you say so."

"I do."

* * *

Bo

Christmas bingo. Two words I never thought I'd say together in my life and yet here I was actually playing it. So sue me, I went back on my word and participated in playing a game. A Christmas one, nonetheless. But what else was I supposed to do? Be the only one not playing? That seemed silly.

And the truth was I wasn't hating bingo. In fact, I thought I was rocking it.

I elbowed Izzy next to me, who missed one, and pointed to the square. "Carolers," I whispered, smiling at her.

In a daze, her eyes glazed over, and she looked up and over at me. "Huh? Oh, yeah." She swiped her marker across the square. "Thanks."

I nodded and quickly marked off another one on my boards as Jesse called it. One more to go and I'd win.

Then he pulled another strip of paper from the bowl. "Reindeer," he called, but I didn't have it, so I checked Izzy's because for all intents and purposes, I'd sworn she checked out. She smiled at me when I marked her board, and all I wanted to do was know what was going on inside that head of hers. I would've thought this would be right up her alley.

"Bingo!" someone sitting on the floor by the fireplace called out and jumped up.

Man, so close!

Everyone started standing and Phil walked over to me. We'd been talking earlier, he was a nice guy. "Who would've guessed a city slicker like you would be so into Christmas bingo," he joked. "I saw you checking your boards like your life depended on it."

"Turns out I like bingo." I laughed at his expression and slapped him on the back. "Come on, let's get another glass of eggnog. Another thing I never would've thought I'd like."

"Good, I want to hear more about that business you were talking about investing in."

Nodding, I followed him over to the kitchen and swiped a peppermint brownie on my way past the dessert table. "You got it!"

* * *

Izzy

Putting aside the fact that I was falling down a rabbit hole, I didn't think I could stop myself even if I wanted to.

I knew I'd been denying it to quite literally everyone that said I was interested in Bo, but maybe they were right. Well, obviously they were right because every time I was around him, it was starting to become more difficult to ignore this feeling that I got. It was like I wanted to be noticed by him, wanted him to see me and smile, something he rarely did around anyone else.

It wasn't fair for me to be feeling this way—neither to him nor myself. I couldn't be catching any feelings for this man. He belonged in New York and wouldn't be happy in a town like this, and I loved this town and couldn't see myself anywhere else.

Ugh, but if that was the case, then why couldn't I stop this nagging feeling in my chest, this giddy feeling I got whenever he looked at me tonight? And what was that about during bingo? I'd never have thought that Bo would look at me that way, but he did. He looked at me like I was special to him, like I mattered to him.

Maybe I was overthinking it, I thought, but then I couldn't stop replaying the moment. Forget the fact that he was actually playing one of the very games he refused to play. No, it was all about the way he was acting—his smile, the little looks he sent my way. Like when he whispered the word "carolers" to me.

Maybe he didn't even realize he was doing it.

Maybe he didn't notice the mixed signals he was sending me.

But it was driving me nuts trying to figure out this. . . this. . .

"Izzy," Bo's voice broke me out of my reverie. I turned and watched him stand behind me, his arms wrapping around me. "It's chillier than usual. What are you doing standing out here? You could get sick before the wedding."

I didn't need to look at him to see the concern on his face because I heard it in his voice. See, this was what I was talking about. It was like Bo wanted everyone to see him as some sort of beast, some man to not feel comfortable around. But people were. I was. I was so undeniably comfortable around him.

Sure, he had this icy exterior, but when you got to know him, really got to see within, there was nothing that was stopping me from wanting to know even more about him, everything about him, really.

I cleared my throat and did what I'd been doing best, masking my feelings, burying them deep down. I lifted my chin and tried to act casual, like his arms being around me had no effect on me whatsoever. Not that he'd notice anyway, though, because he was too busy being upset about where he was, the time of year, and why he was here. No doubt he was doing this because he was loyal to Louie, but besides that, please, the entire notion of a wedding was something he disliked. Need I remind you of the cake tasting?

He belonged in New York where he could work tirelessly at a desk in an environment he knew and appreciated. I was right before, and I needed to remember that—it was useless of me to feel anything for Bo because it wouldn't go anywhere.

"You should head back inside, then. You wouldn't want to catch a cold before the wedding and show up as Rudolph." I tried making a joke, but I didn't have it in me to actually deliver it properly, so it fell flat.

He squeezed my sides and peered over my shoulder, looking at me. "*We* should go inside."

Geez, the way he said that one little word—we. My heart was confused. As if almost on instinct, I leaned my head back on him, but it lasted barely a millisecond before he pulled away, leaving my body cold from the lack of his touch, and my head to bob backward before I caught myself and stood up straight again, turning to face him now.

His look was all the reminder I needed to stop myself from misreading the situation. He shoved his hands in his pockets and seemed to regain his composure (read: grumpy demeanor) as he stood opposite of me. "So what's going on? You seem off."

Of course, *that* he picked up on. Give him twenty minutes and maybe, just maybe, he'd pick up on the fact that leaving me hanging when I went to lean into him left me feeling like a grade-A idiot.

I plastered on a phony smile, though, not wanting to get into the thick of things with him. "What do you mean? I'm happy as ever." That was believable, right?

He cocked a brow, clearly not buying it. "I've seen you smile a million times before. I know when it's forced."

I licked my lips, not liking how well he could read me. "Well, you're wrong."

Neither of us said anything, just stood there. Until finally, Bo announced, "All right, well, I'm going inside."

"Okay." Don't let the door hit you on the way in, I thought to myself, as he turned to leave.

Geez, why was I acting like this? Oh, that was right, because I didn't know how else to act since I only seemed to want one thing right now—his arms around me again. And we both knew that wasn't happening.

Hating myself for somewhat losing myself and my usual cheery outlook, I took a deep breath in and then exhaled before stopping him. "Thank you for coming with me tonight."

He didn't turn around, just replied from the doorway, "You're welcome."

Knowing he was only going to walk away at this point, I turned back around, looking out toward the street, at all the cars that were out there. So many people had shown up to this party and it only reminded me how foolish I was being. Yes, Bo was. . . special, but he was also not from around here and had no intention of calling Silver Springs home. I needed to remember that. What I had here was also special. This place was my home.

It was all this wedding planning, it was starting to get to me, causing me to be confused. I needed to get my emotions in check and stop my feelings from getting away from me, so as I stepped through the door and shut it behind me, I tried my hardest to leave it all behind, too.

Chapter Ten

Bo

"I was thinking of adopting a polar bear."

I didn't think too much about Louie's statement, just focused on the game of eight-ball we were playing. With the stick lined up to the five ball, I angled it just right so when I hit the ball it flew into the pocket in Louie's corner.

Then I walked around the table and studied how I needed to angle the stick to get my last one in before aiming for the black ball and winning this game. "Good for you, man," I replied, still not sure why he was adopting a polar bear. It seemed a bit out of the blue to me, but whatever.

He moved around the table now, too, and placed a hand on the top of his stick before pointing to my ball. "Are you sure you want to try for that pocket?"

I blew outward and gave him my full attention now, pausing and leaning my stick against the wall as I crossed my arms. "All right, that does it. What's going on?"

Let me explain because you don't have the full story here. See, Louie was finally back in town through the new year—no more traveling, aside from his honeymoon. He invited me over to his place for beers and a guys' night of shooting some pool. It was exactly what I was hoping we'd have time to do before his wedding.

But ever since I got here he'd talked about the weirdest (read: most random) stuff. At first, it was Santa's tracker games online, then some app he found that could name a star after Fiona, a place in Nantucket he saw in a brochure, and now this. . . adopting a polar bear. So now you can see why I was right and truly baffled, especially when we were playing such a good game.

"What?" Louie shrugged, acting like he had no clue what I was talking about. "The polar bear would be for Fiona, not me." *Not the point.* "She's all for protecting nature and this is a good cause. Did you know that—"

I put a hand up. "Dude, I don't care about fast facts about polar bears or any other species if that's where this is going."

He sighed and shook his head, his gaze dropping to his shoes. "I can't do this. I'm sorry."

"What are you talking about?" I was no therapist, but even I could see all this blabber was really about something else entirely. "Are you nervous about the wedding?" I hedged because that would make sense to me.

"What?" he asked, sounding incredulous. "No way, it's not that."

"Then what's going on because I thought we were playing pool, but it seems like you have something else on your mind."

"Fiona asked me to try to get you to talk about Izzy, that's why I keep bringing up stuff that leads back to women, um, Izzy," he explained and leaned against the table, crossing his arms now, too. "But I'm no good at this chick stuff, sorry, so let's just pretend I did what she asked and you told me about Izzy."

I felt like I was talking to Lassie. "What about Izzy?"

"I don't know, Fiona heard Izzy was helping you enjoy Christmas again and I know that topic is off limits, so. . . ."

I exhaled and looked around the room. *Was I being pranked?* "You brought up Christmas within the first ten minutes with that Santa tracker stuff. Which, by the way, who cares about that anyway? It's not like you and Fiona have kids or anything. What, you mean to tell me you play that stupid game for fun?"

He flipped me the bird. "Some of us actually like the holidays."

"I don't mind them," I mumbled.

"Since when?" he grumbled, giving me a yeah-right look and tapped the edge of the table. "You're like a real-life Scrooge."

"I'm not that bad," I defended. "And you know I didn't grow up in a town centered around mistletoe and tinsel like you did."

"What can I say?" He shrugged his shoulders. "I'm just that cool."

"Or lame," I disputed.

"Whatever, dude." Then he spat out, "Why don't you just put us both out of our misery and answer the question—what's going on with you and Izzy and apparently Christmas now?"

Truth was, I really didn't want to talk about Izzy. "Well, I don't think she and I are anywhere close to adopting a polar bear, but maybe a blue-footed booby. They need saving, too, you know?"

He smirked, understanding me and my intention to avoid answering his question directly. Izzy and I were friends, I supposed you could say, so wasn't that enough? It was a ton more than I thought we'd ever be when we first met.

Playing along now, he replied, "Sounds good. Just make sure you work out who's getting the plush one on the weekends. When you adopt, you only get one, you know. That can cause a tricky custody arrangement."

I didn't see why we had to go talking about this, even if his soon-to-be wife put him up to it. This wasn't some love song or something. I didn't write in a diary and, frankly, I had nothing to say. There was nothing going on between Izzy and me. "If you need to tell Fiona something, you can tell her this," I paused before carefully crafting my answer. I didn't want anyone getting the wrong idea. "Izzy isn't as bad as I originally thought."

He nodded. "I can work with this."

As much fun as this was, I raked a hand through my hair and picked up my stick again. "Good. Now are we going to finish this game so I can kick your butt or what?"

Laughing, he answered, "Yeah, yeah, sure."

Pleased, I lined up the stick and was about to hit the ball to win the game when I heard Louie ask, "Wait! Not bad?" just as I made my move.

But his outburst caused me to apply too much pressure.

That was it, all my concentration was lost and the ball hit the wall of the table. It was so far from the hole it wasn't even funny. I cursed under my breath and exhaled. Apparently, this wasn't over and we were going to talk about this some more. Don't get me wrong, I liked hanging out with Louie, he was my best friend for crying out loud, but I didn't care for the third degree.

"Right, that's what I said."

He stared at the table, clearly trying to determine which ball he should try to shoot next, not that his head was in the game. "With all this wedding stuff—thanks again by the way—you've been spending plenty of time together, right, so that's it?"

Fine, he clearly wasn't letting this go, so I'd say it. "Yeah, she's fine. I've never met anyone like her."

But that didn't mean anything.

In fact, it wasn't really saying anything at all if you thought about it.

Technically, the acrobat from the circus I went to when I was a kid wasn't like anyone I'd met before and I wasn't interested in her.

"Okay," Louie replied.

"Okay?"

What the heck? That vague answer did the trick?

I laid my stick down and slumped into one of this leather chairs, determined to forget about the game for now since he obviously wasn't interested in playing anymore. I picked up a beer from his mini fridge and popped the cap.

He nodded and sat down next to me, reaching for his own bottle. "I don't want to pry, just got to keep the fiancée happy." Then he took a swig and added, "But just so you know, Izzy is never leaving this town."

I did a double take. He thought I didn't think that? Of course I knew that. Izzy and this town were like peanut butter and jelly. They didn't have to be together, but when they were, magic happened. But still, I didn't know why he was telling me that. "Why say that?" I asked, cocking a brow.

"I'm just stating facts. If you did want to start dating. . . ."

Oh, so this was where this was going. I wasn't even going to entertain that notion, though, because I never said anything to make him believe I wanted to be with her, did I? Plus, it wasn't like Izzy would be interested in me. And even if she was, it wouldn't last, right? Someone like me didn't land someone like her. No, someone like me ended up alone with nothing but his work to keep him warm at night.

I brushed off his insinuation. "Dude, just stop. You're getting way ahead of yourself. I never said that."

"All right, but don't say I didn't warn you."

Good, but surprisingly I did have one other thing to say on this topic. Just so we all knew where I stood. "I don't hate this town by the way." Louie shot me a look that said don't be an idiot, to which I said, "Well, not as much as I did when I first got here anyway."

"And you're saying Izzy had nothing to do with that?"

I thought back to all of the moments we'd shared since I got here and let them play in mind for the briefest of moments, but then decidedly answered, "Not a thing."

He tilted his head and then shook it. "I know what I'm buying you for Christmas now."

"Oh, please, not another tie. I have enough of those things. And I don't like stripes. I'm not a zebra."

He laughed. "Not a tie. A mirror."

"No, thanks. I already know how handsome I look," I joked. A mirror—that was almost as bad as the gift cards I gave my parents because I had no clue what else to get them.

Now before you go thinking "wow, this Bo guy is a jerk," I wasn't. I mean, sometimes I was. But as far as gift-giving for my parents went. . . I tried, I really did in the past. One year I got my father an antique cigar holder, and sure, he thanked me, but I later found out he gave it to one of his friends from the club. And my mom? Same thing. Anytime I gave her anything, she returned it for something she actually wanted—her words. Just another reason I hated the holidays: expectations were too high and never met. See, not the bad guy.

Louie harrumphed. "You're something else, you know that?" He shook his head. "You should see your face when Izzy's name comes up. Honestly, it's freaky how your expression changes. Almost like a smile is threatening to show up, the corners of your lips tugging up."

I pinched the bridge of my nose. "What, do you think you're like some relationship expert now that you're getting married? We can't all be like you and Fiona, okay? It's great that you're getting married, but it doesn't mean I want to. I'm perfectly content with my life. I'm a freaking CEO, man." I'd been down that road before, I was burned, and I'm not ready to go back down it. No, I was much better suited for business than romance.

Louie popped the cap on a second beer and took another swig. "Fine. Let's change the subject." Then he did. "So how about those polar bears?"

Chapter Eleven

Izzy

Today Santa was coming to my bookstore to read to the children. It was an annual thing and they all seemed to love Jesse, er, Santa. Jesse really got into character and at this point had earned his title of Silver Spring's resident Claus.

Not wanting to wrinkle the Santa suit he dropped off a few days ago in preparation for today's big event, I draped it over the back of the old red velvet throne chair with gold-painted accents I pulled out every year for this event.

Jesse insisted on getting dressed here after last year's debacle. Basically, one of the kids saw Jesse driving over without his beard and then made a whole thing out of it. Kids were freaking out, parents nervous. So yeah, it was safe to say we definitely had to change that this year.

I looked at my watch and realized it was still early, though, so I decided to fix the shelves. Walking over to one in particular, I fussed with my own Santa hat. Yes, I got to wear one, too, as Santa's helper, of course.

At the sound of my door opening, I turned and saw Bo coming in. He was wearing a caramel-colored sweater that showed off his abs and arms. I hadn't seen his arms since he always wore long sleeves, but could only imagine the way they were ripped. As he walked closer, I wanted so badly to break my stare so he didn't notice, but it seemed that wasn't happening. My eyes couldn't help themselves, they continued their descent down. The way his jeans looked so good on him. There was no way, unless you were a Greek god, that you could look this. . . this. . .

Delicious?

No.

Sculpted.

"Hey, Izzy."

I heard the words. I knew they were coming from Bo, but it was like I was in a trance. Well, if a trance meant being totally taken by a man who happened to be leaving town soon and I was never going to see again, at least not for a good long while, then, yes, I was in a trance. And then the realization that we would never have potential to be anything more than friends hit me like a mack truck.

Just like the realization that *maybe*, just maybe I was interested in this man.

Boy, was I in a pickle.

"Izzy," I heard his deep voice say again, obviously trying to get my attention.

At this point, I could've just worn a sign that said: I'm staring at your body and don't want to look elsewhere because you're a beautiful specimen of a man.

Geez, what was wrong with me?

"Yeah," I replied finally, shaking my head and trying my best to play it cool.

The smirk that he was wearing must've meant that he noticed me staring. Oh, who was I kidding, I didn't exactly hide it. That was me, folks, the girl who wore her heart on her sleeve and couldn't seem to not give away the fact that I was attracted to this man.

Any minute now sirens were going to go off. Please evacuate the building everyone, we have a Stage 1 Starer. It was probably just as bad as being a Stage 1 Clinger.

Trying to ignore all that, I gave him a small smile and asked, "What's up?"

Honestly, I was surprised he was here. I didn't think I'd ever see Bo walk into my bookstore—definitely not of his own volition.

He stuffed his hand in his pocket and pulled something out. A little silver bell with a blue ribbon hanging off of it. "The jingle bells came in," he explained, looking at it himself and grinning. "They're nice, right?"

I couldn't believe what I was seeing or hearing, but it seemed Bo was actually fond of a Christmas decoration that we got as favors for Louie and Fiona's joint bach party.

"Festive bells in your pocket," I noted. "Next thing you know you're going to carry candy canes."

He cocked a brow. "I wouldn't go that far. I emailed you about these coming in, though, and didn't hear back from you. I figured you'd want to see how they turned out for yourself."

I reached to take it in my hand as he passed it to me. "Here," he said, handing it over, our fingers grazing, and I looked up into his eyes. He stared back at me and our hands stayed frozen in place for what seemed like a full minute until he finally cleared his throat and backed up slightly.

I took the bell and looked at it closer. "Kissing," I blurted out completely out of the blue. Truthfully, I was just trying to break the awkward silence that was lingering in the air. "They're kissing bells," I told him.

He brought a hand to the back of his neck and looked down. "Right."

"They came out perfect. The initials look great and I really think everyone's going to love them."

"Yeah, I think Louie and Fiona will be happy."

"Of course they will," I guaranteed. "Fiona loves sleigh bells and you said Louie likes mini things like those bottles, so this was kind of genius."

"Sure. You know, I still don't get why they're called kissing bells," he said and all I wanted to do was stare at his lips framed by his beard, my mind obviously hung up on the word kissing. The idea of kissing Bo.

Fighting every instinct, any possibility of experiencing that firsthand, I forced myself to concentrate on his words and put the bell down. "We're going to go over this again?"

He chuckled. "I'm sorry. It's just anytime someone rings this stupid bell they're supposed to kiss? It sounds a little absurd to me. They're silver bells. Everyone knows that. For marketing purposes someone just called them kissing bells and the label stuck. Simple as that."

I couldn't believe this. Well, I could, actually. Bo was a cynic, such a handsome cynic—not the point, my brain screamed—so, it was clear why he wouldn't want to just go with this. Yes, it was just a bell, but wasn't mistletoe just mistletoe until it became tradition to kiss under it?

It was magic.

If there was ever a time to believe, this was it.

Why couldn't he just let go, why couldn't he open himself up—to joy, to possibilities? To me?

Before I could say anything else, whatever I was feeling dissipated with the ringing of my phone, reality coming back down on me.

Bo pinched the bridge of his nose. "Your ringtone is the song from *How the Gri*—" I gasped, causing him to stop talking abruptly. "What?" he asked, furrowing his brows as he looked more confused than ever before. "What's the gasp for?"

I held up a finger and grabbed my phone. "I'm going to answer this, but the fact that you know where that song is from. . . ." I held a hand to my chest and sighed happily. "Oh, Bo, maybe you aren't as bad off as I feared."

Could that mean something?

Could there be hope yet for this grump?

As I clicked into the call, he rolled his eyes and muttered something incoherent. Unfazed, I answered, "Hello?" with an ear-to-ear smile on my face that couldn't be helped. This was a moment I didn't think I'd ever forget. Maybe he didn't like that it was my ringtone, but it was and he knew where it came from.

"Hiya, Izzy. It's Jesse." He didn't need to tell me that. Even though I didn't check the screen before I accepted the call, I already knew it was Jesse. He had a distinct voice that I could pinpoint.

I chuckled. "Jesse, what's going on? Are you on your way?"

Silence.

"Jesse," I pushed. "The silence doesn't bode well with me. What aren't you telling me? What did you call to say?" I began growing nervous. Silence was never good, especially when it was coming over the phone.

"I hate to do this, but I caught whatever Nancy had and won't be able to make it."

I placed my elbows on the counter and knew it was true, I could hear it in his voice. He sounded like he had been put through it.

I ran a hand over my face. "You're kidding me?" I knew he wasn't, just wished it was all some big joke. "It's too late to cancel at this point." I exhaled. "It's fine. It's not your problem, though. Don't worry about it. I'll figure something out. You just get better, okay?"

"I really hate doing this to you. It's tradition."

I nodded. "I know. Next year, though, you'll be right back here. Just worry about you right now, okay? Your health is the most important thing."

"Thanks, Izzy, and I'm sorry again about this."

After I hung up, I stared at my phone, wishing it was indeed a sick joke, that he was outside my store and would come in any minute, laughing at my expense. But that wasn't Jesse. He wouldn't do that to me or the kids and he certainly wouldn't laugh about it.

I started running through the list of potential fill-ins in my head.

"What's the matter?" Bo asked, a hand covering mine now on the counter. "I don't think I've ever seen you like this. It's sort of unsettling, actually."

I looked upward and then back at him. "Jesse can't make it."

"Can't make what?" he asked. "The wedding?"

I shook my head. The thing was, I was a planner and I wished I'd had advanced notice. And I knew that was ridiculous because who planned on getting sick? But still. Now I had no idea what I was going to do.

Without Santa, it was just me reading to the kids. Something told me they didn't want me reading a Christmas story to them.

Ugh, what was the solution?

He began rubbing concentric circles on my hand until I looked down at the way he was trying to calm me down and tilted my head. Was it just me or was Bo being more acute to my feelings than usual?

"Jesse's sick, so he can't be Santa and read to the kids today," I explained to him.

"Oh."

"Yeah."

He shrugged his shoulders. "I'll do it," he said as if it was the most obvious thing in the world.

"You'll do what?" I didn't think I was understanding him. I mean, logic told me that he was offering to step in for Jesse, but Bo volunteering to wear a Santa suit and read to a group of children? Children who believed in the magic of Christmas and that one man could visit every child's home in one single night? No, that couldn't be what he was saying.

"I'll fill in for Jesse."

When I didn't say anything, just stood there, mouth slightly agape, he said in other words, "I'll be Santa."

I shook my head. "I'm sorry. You'll be Santa? As in wear this suit?" I pointed to the suit. "And fake your love for Christmas in front of doe-eyed children?"

He narrowed his eyes. "Don't make me say it again, okay? And you better take me up on the offer before I change my mind."

Without hesitation, I grabbed the Santa suit (hat and all) and shoved it at him. "Thank you for doing this! I'm just going to run to the store and get you a beard. I'll be back in twenty minutes."

* * *

Bo Grant was Santa Claus.

The grumpiest man quite possibly ever was playing the role of the happiest man—well, fictional man—on earth. The world was officially off its axis. Everything as we knew it, folks, was all messed up. Up was down. Down was up.

And Bo was Santa.

Santa = Bo.

Bo = Mr. Claus.

The only problem was, Bo refused to come out of the backroom. "There's no way I'm going out there." He tried crossing his arms like a cool guy and then cursed at all the fabric that was preventing him from doing it. "I take it back. You have to find a new Santa."

I shook my head rapidly. "No way, Bo. It's too late for that now. You have to go out there because if you don't, then I'm going to have a room full of disappointed children." Then I crossed my own arms and arched a brow. "Is that what you want?"

He looked like he was considering my words, but then deadpan returned, "They'll get over it."

I shot him a look. "Bo, you said you'd do it." I half whined on the last part, but I couldn't help it. He couldn't hang me out to dry. Would he do that? I didn't think so, but then again, I'd been wrong before where men were concerned.

And Bo seemed to be full of surprises.

I grabbed his white gloved hands in mine and looked up at him. "Please, Bo. It would mean the world to me."

His expression softened and it was as though I could see the ice melting away from his usual chilly glare. He lifted one of his hands and placed a loose hair behind my ear. "I can't say no to you."

I could feel my cheeks heat up and licked my lips, watching as his hand fell back to mine and he squeezed them. "Don't worry I'll be your Santa."

Whether it was my nerves, I couldn't be sure, but I chuckled. "Great."

Was it just me or was it suddenly stifling in here?

I took my hands and wiped them on my pants, suddenly all too aware of how sweaty my palms felt. "You look jolly." He looked jolly? Where did that come from?

"Thanks?" He cocked a brow and fixed his Santa hat before grabbing his belly under the red coat and yelping, "Ho-ho-ho!"

I smacked my lips together and stifled a laugh. "Go, Santa."

He winked at me and pulled at the elasticity on the white beard covering his own black one so he could whisper, "Watch out, Izzy. If you're not a good girl, you'll get coal in your stocking."

I hung my mouth open as he smacked the beard back in place. "Snow worries. I'm always a good girl."

He gave me a blank expression.

"See what I did there?" I elaborated, "Because it's snow instead of no."

He walked out, shaking his head the entire time. Whatever, it was funny.

"Santa!" I heard being yelled from various voices.

"Oh, ho-ho-ho!" he exclaimed again, this time much louder, though.

I looked upward and closed my eyes. Something told me that was the only thing he knew about Santa.

* * *

"The stockings were hung by the—"

"He's great, isn't he?" Without ever taking my eyes off Bo, I asked Gavin, who was standing to the side of me, his arms crossed as he had a scowl on his face that said: this is the last place on earth I want to be.

But he came because he thought we should go out together and this would convince me it was a good idea. I didn't know how he figured that, but fine.

Gavin sighed. "Sure, if you're actually falling for his act." He turned to me and placed his hands on my arms, like he did the last time he was here. "You should've called me, Izzy. I would've suited up for you." His voice got deeper on that last part as he puffed out his chest.

I glared at his hands on me and then made moves to remove them myself when he clearly wasn't getting the hint. It was probably because his brain couldn't function, since his head was obviously inflated with that ego of his.

"That's very kind of you, but Bo was here and he offered. I think it was a nice gesture, he didn't have to do it." Unlike if Gavin would've done it—that would've come with some obligation on my part. Some obligation I would've never been okay with, mind you, like go out with him.

But unlike Gavin, Bo was unassuming, kinder, gentler even. I knew he didn't want anyone to see that side of him, but I did. I saw the man beneath the beast he wanted everyone to see.

Even now, I looked back at Bo and reveled in the smile he was wearing. It couldn't even be hidden by the snowy white beard. And it looked genuine. If I didn't know any better, I'd think he was actually enjoying himself.

"Please, Izzy, don't honestly tell me you're interested in that guy."

I shrugged. Not that it was any of his business, but, "So what if I am?"

"You can't be. A woman like yourself? You wouldn't last with a man like him. You need a man like me. You're the most beautiful woman in town and if you need a little persuasion, well, I don't mind giving it because I know how great we can be together."

That was it. I invited him here because he was adamant and refused to see that he and I would never be more than mere acquaintances. But it was time Gavin heard me and respected what I wanted.

Not that I knew what that was, but it certainly wasn't Gavin. He had no right to try to control me or make me feel bad for not wanting him. I also could not be convinced.

So I asked Gavin, "What exactly do you mean a man like him? You've said that twice now and I don't think I like what you're implying."

"I'm still implying it."

"Don't." I pointed to the door. "I want you to leave."

"Izzy, don't you think you're overreacting just a little?"

"No, I'm not." Before he turned to leave, I seethed, "And I don't like lobster."

Never had I been so grateful to see someone walk out of my bookstore before. Seeing Gavin walk out of those doors, I realized something.

Bo never had a reason to be any way other than he was, but I knew he was more than he let on. He wasn't grumpy, he wasn't a beast, he was a good man with a good heart. Maybe a few too many lousy experiences, if the childhood he told me about was any indication.

But even that wasn't enough to stop him from helping his friend when he needed it. Just look at what he'd done for Louie, stopping his life to come here to Silver Springs and help with the wedding planning.

And the way he helped me out of a jam today, even though we both knew he would've rather have had a root canal than dress up like Santa and read a story to over a dozen kids who still believed.

Bo was the real deal.

And in that moment, I knew all my friends were right. It was always there, just below the surface. I didn't want Bo to leave. I didn't want whatever chapter we were writing together to end. I wanted it to continue, to grow into more chapters, an entire frigging book.

I wanted it to be a tale as old as time.

Chapter Twelve

Bo

Why were those man's hands on Izzy?

She didn't look happy about it. In fact, quite the opposite, she looked pretty peeved.

That did it, Santa suit and all, I was going over there to help her.

"Santa, you stopped reading. Why?" the little boy in the front row asked, his brown eyes as wide as saucers.

"Sorry, kid."

When I got sour expressions all around, I cleared my throat and got back into character. "Now where were we?" I asked, my voice taking on Santa's deep baritone.

I didn't have much of the story left to read, but I still wasn't focused on the words nearly as much as I should've been. My eyes kept darting over to where Izzy was standing with that guy.

He looked so smug, so arrogant, the way he was looking at her, his chest puffed out, like he thought the sun rose and set with him. Geez, I hated men like him. I especially wasn't fond of him, though, because I had never seen Izzy look as upset as she was in his presence. As she pointed to the door, by way of showing him to it I could only hope, I read the last line in the story aloud. "And to all a good night."

"Is that it?" A little girl pulled at her pigtails. "Can you read us another story, Santa?"

Before I could even answer, I got "pleases" all around from the group of kids, some even with a pout.

"Ho, ho, ho! I wish I could, but—"

"But Santa has to get back to the North Pole. He put the elves in charge while he was gone, but now he has to get back. Right, Santa?" Izzy asked me pointedly as she walked over to join the little rugrats.

"Ho, ho, ho!" I bellowed again, holding onto my stuffed belly and standing. "That's right or they'll elf around and we can't have that, we have toys to deliver soon. Now you all go home and make sure you've sent your lists to me, okay," I said, not sure where that came from, but it seemed to do the trick so I made a beeline for the backroom.

No more than five minutes later, Izzy joined me. I was taking off my white beard and tossing it on a chair to the side where the jacket was already sitting—that was the first thing that went.

"The kids loved you," Izzy said, a smile on her face. Only, this time I didn't mind it as much as I usually did.

Maybe smiles were growing on me.

Maybe Izzy was.

Either way, I scoffed. "Well, I'm done with the Santa gig. I quit, retire, whatever you want to call it. I'm never wearing this thing again." I gestured to the ridiculously bulky ensemble and grunted, pulling the belly stuffing off. "It smells, too."

"No," she said, waving a hand in the air and walking closer. "Plus, I kind of liked the beard. You might want to steal it and take it home to New York. The ladies there might like it, too."

I cocked a brow. "You see I have a beard, right?" I touched my own real one now, glad to be rid of the white long one that was beginning to tickle me. "And mine's not white or forever long and unmaintained. Bonus points in my book."

She gave me a lopsided smile and swayed her head back and forth. "True. I never thought I'd like a man with a beard before. Until you."

I widened my eyes. Like a man with a beard before? Did she like one now? Did she like *me*?

Quickly, she backed up, "I mean, not until yours. And I don't like a man with a beard, well, not like that anyway.

Just that I never liked beards and now I think I do." She cringed as she rambled. "It's not you that I like. Although, I don't dislike you."

I knew what she was saying. I held up a hand to try and put her out of her misery. "It's fine. I understand what you mean."

Sighing, she clasped her hands together and nodded her head toward the door. "Good. Well, I should get back out there. The kids are shopping, so. . . ." she said, her words trailing off.

"Wait," I said, extending a hand to touch her, only I never actually did because she turned around so fast and I dropped my hand.

She gave me a questioning look.

Oh, what was I thinking? That was right, I was thinking I sort of liked this girl and wanted to spend more time with her. Don't worry, I was going to go to the hospital later to get my head checked out.

"Bo?" she pushed. "What is it?"

"The party," I blurted out. "For Louie and Fiona. We should talk about it."

Furrowing her brows, she asked, "Talk about it? What about it?"

Nice going, Bo. You were starting to make no sense. Yes, what did I want to talk about?

All of the details we already covered?

Or how about all of the details we already covered?

Go ahead, you could think it—I was an idiot.

"Just forget it."

"No, it doesn't matter. We can talk about whatever you want. You can come to my house after I close up." She shook her head and chuckled nervously. "I mean, for dinner. I'm heating up leftover soup, so nothing special, but still. It gets lonely sometimes eating alone, so it would be nice to share a meal and we can talk about whatever." Then she placed her hands up. "If you want to, of course."

I didn't know what I wanted anymore. "Sure. Sounds nice." Then out of the blue, I flicked the white ball at the end of her Santa hat and smiled, enjoying the way it looked on her.

* * *

Izzy had never looked at me that way before, the way she just had with a smile that reached her eyes, that seemed to sparkle. And when I placed my hand in the middle of the table, she did the same until our hands were touching. She never attempted to move away, either.

Maybe I was overthinking things and should ignore it. Although, this felt like the first time we were truly seeing one another.

It was nice.

It was also certainly new. Unless it had been brewing from the very start.

"So how did you get to live in a town with sixteen hundred people?" I asked, standing to clear our soup bowls, but she stopped me.

"It's okay."

"I don't mind."

"Neither do I. Please, sit."

"Okay." I sat down again, my gaze turning to her Christmas tree that sat in her living room. It was exactly what I'd expect from this woman—big, festive and cheerful.

"Anyway, it's sixteen hundred and two," she corrected me before answering my question. "And I grew up here. This town is all I've ever known."

"Wow, well, the two additional people change everything. I was wrong. This isn't a small town. This is a great big town." We both laughed. "It's just. . . I can't see how anyone would want to stay here. Didn't you ever want to leave?"

She shrugged and took a sip of her water. "You know, in high school all I heard was about how everyone couldn't wait to graduate so they could get out of here. They swore they'd never come back once they left and some of them haven't." She sighed. "But for me, I couldn't imagine a better place to call home. Sure, it's small, but I have everything I need right here."

"Do you think you'll ever want to travel, see the world?"

"No, I don't think so. I want a family. I want to settle down and get married, actually. I want children, a full house to share my joyful and woeful days with. Isn't that what life is all about? Being able to share in the good and bad times?"

"Seems like you believe in happily ever after."

"You don't?"

"I believe in reality," I said, sighing.

At her pout, I knew I couldn't just leave it at that. And maybe Izzy was the first person in my life, besides Louie, who I considered a friend, someone I could talk to. I ran a hand through my hair and leaned back. "It's just that I didn't have the greatest childhood and my parents didn't have the best marriage. I don't even think I'd know the first thing about being someone's husband, let alone a father one day. See, the thing is, I'm good at business. I know what I'm doing when it comes to negotiations and board meetings. Family life, not so much."

"Does anyone really know anything? You learn as you go. That's what we're all doing, really. We're learning and making mistakes as we go." She leaned forward, her arm coming across the table, her chest pushed up against it. The Christmas music she had on in the background changed to a more upbeat song.

I tried to listen to the lyrics, but found myself thinking aloud. "I don't like to make mistakes."

"Did you know everything about business right out of the gate? I'm sure you didn't, but you learned and now you love it because you feel comfortable doing it."

I nodded. "I suppose."

Why was it that this woman had a tendency to make me think about things I usually didn't think about?

* * *

"I don't believe it," I said, shaking my head in denial as I wiped the pot she heated our soup in, Izzy next to me at the sink with rubber gloves and suds up to her elbows as she washed the dishes.

"Well, believe it," she replied, her voice full of laughter. "I ate all the garland and had no clue what to say when my teacher asked me where it went."

"In your stomach?"

"It was popcorn and cranberry garland. No teacher should trust a ten-year-old with that."

"And yet your peers didn't eat it."

"Hey! Some of them did." Full of laughter at the memory, Izzy pointed a sudsy finger in my direction. "Don't judge! Anyway, it happened to be taco Tuesday. I never did like taco Tuesday. Worst day of the week in my book."

Astonished by this fact, I stood there, my mouth hanging open. "What? Who hates tacos?" I'd never heard of anyone saying no to tacos, let alone hating them.

"Me." She laughed, the sound washing over me like a warm hug. It wasn't the first time she'd laughed tonight and I was quickly realizing I liked it. "Well, when I was a kid. Now they're just fine."

"Just fine? That's what you say about broccoli or peas."

"Don't like green veggies, do you?" she countered passing me a teacup to dry.

"Not when I was a kid. But I was more normal than you. Tacos." I scoffed. "That's like a crime or something to not love tacos at any age."

I ran my cloth over the delicate object and moved to grab the handle, but it slipped from my big hands before I could get a grip on it and it hit the floor square on its side.

"Oh tinsel!" Izzy cried out.

"I'm so sorry," I rushed to say, feeling useless. "I don't usually have butter fingers. I don't know what happened."

"It's fine, really. It fell out of your hands. It's not your fault. These things happen," she said looking at the floor as I bent down to pick it up for her.

I held it out as she slipped off her gloves. "It's broken," I said, sounding lame even to my own ears. Of course it's broken, it wasn't rubber.

Looking at it, she spun it in her hands until her finger connected with the now missing piece. "It's not broken per say. Just chipped."

"Same thing."

"No, it's okay."

I shook my head. Wasn't she going to get mad or make me feel bad? "You're not upset?"

Still holding it, she reached for the broken piece on the floor. "It's not ideal, but it's just a cup."

"You're not actually going to keep this and drink out of it, are you?"

"No, of course not. But it's nice. I actually think I like it chipped."

"You like a chipped cup?" I did not understand this woman. How could everything always be so bright in her world? What was wrong with me that I wasn't more like that?

Oh, that was right—life jaded me.

"Nothing's perfect, Bo. This just reminds us of that."

Exactly! Like life, my brain shouted at me. But why did that have the kind of effect it did on me and not her? Not sure I wanted to vocalize my thoughts, instead I said, "I certainly don't need a reminder of that. I know nothing is perfect."

"Maybe so, but it's imperfectly perfect if you ask me." She smiled and walked the cup to a cabinet where she set it behind the glass on full display. Then she turned to me and winked.

Unable to stop myself, I smiled, too. I still felt bad, but there was something about her response to the whole thing that just surprised me, made me feel a little bit better. "Then that's all that matters."

Breaking eye contact, she walked back to the sink. "You know, I really should finish cleaning up. You don't have to keep drying."

"What, do you not trust me? I wouldn't, either." Obviously I couldn't be trusted.

"No, I just think you're a guest. You shouldn't have to keep working with me," she said.

"You said that before."

"It's okay, I have this under control," she said all but ushering me out. "Look, why don't you sit down in the living room and enjoy a good book."

I turned to the shelf she had lining the wall opposite of her tree. "Like read one?"

She nodded. "I'll be right out and I can join you, unless you want to leave." She bit her bottom lip as she waited for my decision.

"I'll read, thanks."

* * *

I looked over at Izzy who was curled up next to me on the couch, her feet underneath her. After she finished cleaning up, she came and sat down next to me, fully intending on reading, too, but she obviously fell asleep.

I lifted the book from her hands—her grip on it loose at best—closed it and laid it down on the end table. Waking her was the last thing I wanted, especially when she looked so peaceful, but it was late and I figured I should probably get going.

Before I could move, though, she stirred next to me then opened her eyes and pulled back to look at me. "Sorry, I fell asleep."

"It's okay," I said, patting her knee. "It's late. I should go."

Nodding, she sat up straighter. "Yeah, okay. Thanks for letting me sleep."

"I guess I got a little absorbed in the fictional world." I held up the book I was reading.

Smiling, she fixed her hair and extended her feet out in front of her. "Did you finish it?"

I shook my head. "No, but if it's all right with you, I think I'll keep it here. Maybe I can finish it another time." That would mean I'd have to come back.

Only, what would happen when I went back to New York? My time here was almost up. Would we get another night like this?

How I hoped so.

It turned out, I rather enjoyed myself today, spending time with Izzy was getting a lot more enjoyable for me. Looked like things weren't so cut and dry, after all. I certainly had some thinking to do. I needed to learn to have more balance in my life, not make it all about work. Just look at how nice things were when I wasn't working twenty-four seven.

As if reading my mind, Izzy said, "If you change your mind, you can always come back and take it with you."

"Thanks." I stood up and put the book back where it belonged on her shelf, deciding I needed to leave now before I did something stupid.

But she stopped me—"Hey, Bo?"

"Yeah?" I asked, turning back around.

"I had a nice time," she said softly, a smile coloring her expression.

Something inside of me stirred and I felt it to my very core. This woman, this town, it was all changing me. I never expected any of this. Not after years of being shut off from all human emotion. The worst part, I didn't mind it. "I did, too," I returned, acknowledging her words.

There was something about Izzy Monroe that was as bright and special as that great, big Christmas tree she had sitting in her living room. She was like the light to my darkness, the optimism to my realism. In that moment, I knew I liked everything about her, especially the world she lived in, the way she saw it.

Too bad we were from two different worlds and I wasn't sure I could leave mine. I'd been a resident of it for far too long.

Could I make the change?

Or would I sour her? That was something I never wanted, not for her.

"Goodnight, Izzy," I said, my thoughts getting to me, and opened her front door with a final wave goodbye.

I wasn't sure why, but my heart felt heavy. Like I was walking away from my best friend. What was going on with me?

Chapter Thirteen

Izzy

"On your mark, get—"

Zel bursted out laughing, her hyena laugh coming out strong. That sound only came out when she was really laughing, like laughing so hard she couldn't contain herself.

Fiona chuckled and looked pointedly at Zel who was supposed to be starting the race, but this was her second attempt at it and every time she got to this point, she couldn't stop laughing.

"Maybe we should just skip this game," Bo brought up for the third time.

The first time was when Zel announced the next game— Race You Down the Aisle.

The second was when we partnered off and I wrapped the garter around our ankles.

And the third, well, the third was now when we were about ready to start.

Zel was in charge of coming up with game ideas for Fiona and Louie's joint bach party, so I didn't know why she was finding this amusing. Maybe it was the fact that she was hosting the games. Maybe it was because Louie's other groomsmen couldn't make it so Zel couldn't participate since there was no partner for her. Or maybe it was because there was a row of people standing in front of her coupled off all wearing garters around their ankles—think three-legged race style.

Either way, Fiona blew bubbles. "Can we get on with it already?"

Louie patted her back. "Come on, Zel. I want to show these losers that my fiancée and I are going to kick their butts at this game."

Bo snickered. "Oh, yeah? Like you kicked our butts at the ring hunt?"

To bring you up to speed, he was referring to the game we played before this one. The objective was to find the most toy rings that were hidden around the house—Zel's house, actually. Needless to say, Bo was slightly more competitive than I would've pegged him to be, at least when it came to silly bachelor/bachelorette games.

"You're so going down," Louie went on. "Right, Fiona?" He angled his head toward her. "They're going to eat our dust."

"My competitive fiancé, ladies and gentlemen," Fiona exclaimed, chuckling. "Not everything's a competition, babe."

He gave her a crooked expression, like he was just seeing this lax side of her. "This is a game, sure, but what's the point in playing if you're not going to win?"

Bo nudged my arm. "Don't worry, Izzy, we got this in the bag."

"I'm not worried," I assured him. Then I looked at the finish line ahead and grimaced. "I've got my eye on the prize."

"There is no prize for the individual games," Zel reminded, "only the one with the most cumulative points wins."

I cracked my neck and then the knuckles on my fingers. "Let's do this!" I shouted, which caused everyone to stare in my direction.

Bo flicked one of my antlers from the reindeer headband the bride's squad was wearing. "Easy there, Rudo—"

"Don't you dare call me by the wrong reindeer name again," I mock-seethed, "I'm Dasher."

"Right," he said, then looked at Zel. "Can we finally start, please?"

"Sure," she said, throwing her hands up. "We've wasted enough time. Go!"

What? Now?

Bo started without me and obviously that wasn't going to do the trick because we both went down, falling flat on the floor. Didn't he know this was about teamwork?

"Nice going," he mumbled. "Now Louie has a lead on us!"

"What is it with you two?" I asked as he helped me up.

"Just let's go!" He slipped an arm around my waist, as if prepared to drag me if he had to.

Starting again, we were in third place but just about to get out ahead of the couple in second place, leaving just Louie and Fi we had to beat. They were insanely good at this, though, like they'd been practicing or something. Maybe that was what Bo and I should've been doing.

"Hey, Fi," I called out and she turned around, giving Louie no time to pause, too, and they both went down.

Bo eyed me and smiled, obviously pleased with my devious ways. What, I liked to win, too. And it worked because that little maneuver gave Bo and I enough lead time to cross the finish line and—

"We have a winner!" Zel called out. "Congrats, Bo and Izzy!"

Bo grabbed my hand and held it up high. "Heck yeah we won!"

He was thrilled, like so over the moon happy, I never would've thought I'd see the day. Turned out, winning really put him in a good mood. You'd think he was told he cured cancer or something by how happy he was. Utterly triumphant.

As everyone started taking off the garters, Bo whispered, "Sophomore year in college. Beer pong. It was a nasty, competitive game and he won. Only, I swore he didn't. I still think he cheated. The other guys in the house watching swore he didn't, but I called bull."

I nearly choked. "Wait!" I threw a hand up, calling time out. "You were a frat boy?"

He shrugged and nonchalantly replied, "Yeah. It was no big deal." But that felt like something to be anything but nonchalant about. I mean, had he seen himself? This man did not scream frat boy. I couldn't have been more surprised.

Sharing this, I swatted his arm. "I never would've guessed."

"What did you peg me for?"

I stared at him and smirked. "Honestly, I don't know, but not that. I guess I don't see you as a college kid at all, you're just so. . ." I searched for the right word, but came up short. "So. . ."

"What?" He cocked his brow.

"I don't know. . . mature?"

Laughing now, his smile couldn't be helped and I loved it—the way he looked so happy. "Mature? I'll take that."

"Hmm. Maybe it's the whole soon-to-be CEO thing."

"Maybe." He spun the garter around his finger in the air. "My turn, let me do you."

I crossed my arms, fully prepared for whatever he was going to say—as long as it was kind. "Go for it."

He narrowed his eyes, deep in thought, as he gave me a once-over. "Never late to class, if you could help it. Didn't attend ragers, unless it wasn't a school night. On all the committees that were about school spirit. Befriended everyone, even the nerdy kid who drank chocolate milk with his pizza. Had a massive crush on a jock who wouldn't give you the time of day."

I pursed my lips and nodded, biting back a laugh. "You're almost right."

"Tell me," he commanded, his deep voice obviously curious now.

I caught the garter he was spinning in the air and stretched at the elastic. "I didn't go to college."

"So how was I almost right?"

"That was me in high school," I explained. "Except the jock did give me the time of day, at least until we broke up after prom because he was going to school in California and I was staying here," I said matter-of-factly, feeling mighty good about that one. So good, in fact, that I didn't mind walking away from Bo, leaving him there with what had to be a slew of unanswered questions.

* * *

"Who made the first move?"

Zel was currently hosting the game Shoe on the Other Foot. Don't ask me why it was called that because technically they did swap shoes, but they were holding them up, not placing them on their feet. Anyway, that aside, Fiona and Louie looked like they were having a good time. Well, as good a time as two people could have when they'd been sitting in chairs with their backs toward one another for the past five minutes.

We were all sitting on the sidelines placing bets on who knew each other more.

So far everyone thought Fiona knew Louie more.

But I happened to know Fiona, and she didn't listen as well as you'd think she did.

In fact, for as little as men were known to listen, Fiona listened less than that. Especially when she had something on her mind and, because her job was so demanding, she almost always had something on her mind.

Not that she didn't pay attention when you were talking, but oh you knew what I was saying.

Bo tilted his head downward and whispered in my ear. "They're both too conceited to play this game."

I chuckled, looking over at him. "You're right. They're both going to say it was themselves."

"But really it was—"

"Fiona," Bo cut me off, finishing my sentence.

Zel tossed the cards she was holding with the questions on the floor. "That's it. You two are ridiculous. It's like you're not playing the game right on purpose."

Did I mention Zel was slightly dramatic?

Fiona shot up and gasped when she saw Louie not holding her ballerina flat up. "This is ridiculous." She grabbed the shoe and gave him his back. "You should've been waving this thing in the air."

He guffawed. "Babe, it was me. I made the first move, don't you remember?"

"No, I don't remember and why would I? Because you're making that up."

Louie put his shoe on and blew bubbles. "I don't believe this."

As they tried to figure things out, everyone began walking around and going off to their own corners, talking, otherwise ignoring them—they did this, it'd blow over.

I looked for Zel, but she was nowhere to be found.

"So?" I rocked on the balls of my feet and smacked my lips together, turning to Bo. "This was definitely one of the more interesting bach parties I've been to."

Bo nodded. "Me, too. Although, I liked it better than the usual go to a bar and get too drunk to remember the stripper's name."

I laughed. "Bo Grant letting loose?" I held a hand to my chest and shook my head, trying to contain more laughter. "It just seems wrong."

He scratched his chin, looking like he was clearly feeling —arrogant. "Get your laughs in all you want, but need I remind you I was in a fraternity?"

I scoffed. "What does that mean?"

He gave me a look that said you know what that means. "Frat boys are known to be extremely fun."

"And dumb," I pointed out, actually pointing a finger at him.

He brushed me off. "Whatever."

"So what happened to that guy? When I first met you, I would've never guessed you even knew the definition of a good time."

"I know how to have fun and let loose, but I also know that it's all just a fantasy. When you get back to reality, it's harsh and there's no time or room for fun."

"Because you make it that way."

"No, Izzy, because life is that way."

"I don't believe you think that. I think that deep down you want someone to prove you wrong. And I think that this town is doing that and it scares you."

"I'm not scared," he countered, crossing his arms stiffly.

"Oh, no, I would never say that. Mr. Grumpy himself scared?" I shook my head. "Couldn't be."

"You think I'm grumpy?"

"I think you act like you're a grump, but that's not who you are. I think it's a defense mechanism."

"So what if it is?" he asked me seriously. "You can't change me, Izzy. Not anymore than I can stop you from being all sunshine and rainbows."

I sighed. "I told you, you bring that out in me to overcompensate. That's not who I really am, no more than being like that is who you are. Besides, I don't want to change you. What if I said I like you just the way you are, Bo?"

"Even if I'm grumpy?"

I raised an eyebrow and decided to push him a little. "In spite of that."

"Hey!" he cried, nudging me with his elbow, that smile I enjoyed so much back on his lips.

* * *

Now that the party had pretty much died down, Fiona, Zel, Stassia, Belle and I all took to one of the bedrooms where we piled on the bed, or in Fiona and Belle's case on the love seat near the window.

"All right, I don't know about you guys, but I am beat." Zel tucked her feet under her and sighed. "Who knew celebrating you and Louie would tucker me out so much?" she directed her question toward Fiona.

Fiona closed her eyes and smiled. "It all came together really nice and I couldn't have done any of that without you or Izzy."

I waved a hand in the air, clutching the pillow against me when I brought my hand back down. "Don't even mention it."

"Seriously, don't," Zel warned. "The last thing I want is people asking me to help plan theirs." She shuddered, slightly dramatic about the whole thing. "I couldn't even fathom doing this again."

"What about when it's yours or one of ours?" Stassia asked, a brow hitched in the air. When no one responded, just looked around, Stassia pushed, "Oh, come on! Like you've never considered it before? It could happen, you know. Especially for you."

Belle exhaled and saved Zel from answering because she said, "I, for one, don't plan on settling down anytime soon." Then she added, "We're young. We're beautiful. It would be a sin to take ourselves off the market just yet."

I giggled. "She's right, you know. But that doesn't mean I haven't thought about it."

"It being settling down?" Fiona checked.

I nodded. "Yeah, and it seems pretty nice, actually. I want what you and Louie have."

Stassia was lying on her stomach now, kicking her feet in the air on the bottom of the bed. "I want it," she said earnestly. "Bad," she drew out the word. "It's been my dream since I was a little girl, actually, to be swept off my feet by a handsome prince."

"Seems like just that," Zel interjected, "a dream."

I nudged her side. "Hey, where's this coming from?" I chuckled. "You have men lined up to go on dates with you. Or at least you would if you didn't turn most of them down."

Zel played with the bottom of her long blonde hair. "None of them are the one for me."

I scoffed. "Please, you don't even give them a chance. You make them all casual."

"Wrong move," Belle replied. "Then they get the wrong idea."

"Maybe that's the idea I want them to get," Zel challenged.

Fiona gasped and nearly jumped out of her seat, pointing at Zel now. "Oh my goodness, I don't know how we didn't see it before."

"See what?" Zel asked, her eyebrows furrowing as she looked just as confused as I felt.

What was Fiona talking about?

"You did love someone once and you thought they were the one for you, so now you don't give anyone else a chance," Fiona explained, leaning back and nodding. "I'm right, aren't I?"

Belle swatted her arm. "No one likes a know-it-all."

Fiona just grinned, though, clearly pleased with herself.

"Is that true?" I looked at Zel who was biting her lower lip. If I learned anything from spending time with Bo, it was how the past did have a way of impacting the future, so this could very well be accurate, but only Zel could confirm that.

Zel got off the bed and leaned against the wall as she looked at all of us. "Geez, there are way too many eyes on me right now." Sighing, she started, "So what if it is true? But I don't even know if it was love or what it was." She slid down the wall and sat on the floor, taking her reindeer headband off and placing it beside her. "I was sixteen. I barely knew who I was, let alone what love felt like." But she sighed happily as she looked downward and seemed to begin reliving those days in her head. "He was my older brother's best friend and way out of my league. He'd always been there. Honestly, he was more like a friend, I guess you could say."

"That sounds sweet," Stassia interjected. "What's his name?"

Zel snapped out of the past, though, and came back to the present real soon with that question. "It doesn't matter because we haven't spoken in years."

"Is he still friends with your brother?" Belle asked.

Zel shrugged. "I think so, but I asked him never to tell me about he-who-shall-not-be-named."

"What happened with you two that he can't be named?" Stassia quickly swallowed hard, looking like she wanted to take the words back. She shook her head. "Never mind. Tell us whenever you're ready."

"Yeah," I agreed, knowing my friend and how she'd need that kind of space. "We're here whenever you want to talk."

Zel got up now, came back over, and bounced back on the bed, causing the spring to make noises before she settled on it again, her feet under her in her usual way. "So when are you going to be ready to dish?" She looked pointedly at me and then widened her eyes and let her mouth hang open. "Please, girl, don't even try and pretend that I'm being presumptuous." She pointed a finger in my face. "You know exactly what I'm talking about."

Fi cleared her throat from where she was sitting and coughed, "Bo," before chuckling.

I rolled my eyes and chucked the pillow at her. "There's nothing to tell."

"You're lying," Stassia said, pointing to my forehead and leaning in to touch it. "You're getting this wrinkle on your forehead."

I swatted her hand away. "Am not." I licked my lips, debating on what to say. "There's not much to say, that's all."

"Not much to say or not much you want to say?" Zel pushed.

And wasn't I the one who just said she didn't have to tell us everything now that we'd be here when she was ready?

Well, I wasn't. Ready, that was.

I needed time to figure my feelings out on my own before involving my amazingly nosey friends. I loved them, I really did, but the invasion was a lot sometimes.

"I'm not saying anything more than this: I think I'd be open to see what's between us, if Bo wanted to give it a shot."

After a round of ooo-la-las, I decided to add, "I've been getting to know him more and more and I like him."

"What the elf! I knew you'd like him!" Fiona clutched her chest, looking triumphant.

Of course, she did. That explained so many of the ways she tried to push us together over her wedding planning. And apparently, it worked.

Belle laughed. "I feel like we're in middle school again. Are you two sitting in a tree?"

We all laughed and I rolled my eyes at her. "Real mature."

"Are you two going to the tree lighting together?" Zel asked, her eyes growing wide. "That could be the perfect place to have your first kiss." Then she backed up. "You haven't kissed yet, right? I want to know what its like with his beard," she said, biting on her thumbnail.

"With the beard, we might've just elevated things to high school, maybe college," Belle said, obviously still amused.

Skipping over my sassy friend's remark, I answered Zel's question. "No! Of course not."

Stassia leaned forward, a blush on her cheeks. "I don't know why not. I would've welcomed a little beard burn from that hunk of a man."

I took a pillow from behind me and swatted her with it. "Find your own man who can give you beard burn."

Stassia gasped. "Are you saying he's yours?"

Belle chuckled. "Oh, no. I think you've got it worse than you think, Izzy."

"Excuse me, but I just think it's weird for Stassia to be talking about beard burn like it's sexy."

"Izzy," Zel said, leaning in and practically whispering, "any mark from a man who claims you is sexy."

I smacked my tongue on the roof of my mouth. Leave it to Zel to think that.

Chapter Fourteen

Bo

For the better part of an hour, Izzy and I had been standing back, watching what felt like all sixteen hundred town residents (sorry, sixteen hundred and two) come out and adorn the Christmas tree in the center of town with their personalized Christmas ornaments.

Finally, I couldn't take it anymore, so I turned to Izzy. "Are you going to hang yours yet?"

With a goofy grin on her face, she turned to me. "I think so and I know just the spot." She reached out and took my hand with her free one, the other clutching her ornament to her chest. "Come with me," she explained.

Nodding, I walked with her up to the tree and actually felt the whole community thing she tried to tell me about on more than one occasion. Don't get me wrong, at first I thought it was all malarkey, but seeing the way everyone came out for the event, it was something else. "This is nice," I admitted as we stopped squarely in front of the spot she'd been eyeing.

"It's a good spot, isn't it?"

I wasn't talking about that, but I nodded my agreement just the same.

She dropped my hand and wrapped both hands around her ornament, spinning it around so I could finally get a good look at the thing. It was hand-painted with a red and yellow diamond behind her name, the lettering big and blocky. It was easily one of the nicest (read: not tacky) ornaments I'd seen in my life.

Izzy held up the hook and opened it a bit before slipping it on a branch and closing the hook around it. The way her face lit up as her name blended on the tree among the names of so many others—Nancy, Mike, Lola, Evan—made me think about what it'd be like to see my name someplace like this. In New York that was never happening, but this town had this way about it. Even though I fought it—hard—it sucked me in.

"It's perfect," I noted, my eyes on her again. I mean, nothing was perfect, and yet some things just felt that way, Izzy included.

Murmuring her agreement, she backed up and extended her hand again for me to take. "Want to go find a place to sit and watch the lights go on?" she asked, looking up at the sky. "Once the sun sets, they'll turn them on."

"I'd like that," I said, finding I really meant it. Taking her hand in mine, something we'd been doing lately, I led us away from the tree just as Louie and Fiona were walking up to it, a crowd of others behind them. They looked like two lovebirds who'd be married in less than twenty-four hours, leading the pack, so other than a passing smile, we didn't stop them and kept going.

* * *

Izzy wrapped her hands around the cup of hot cocoa like it was a life raft and she didn't want to let it go because her life depended on it. "Your cup called, it asked that you loosen your grip on it."

She whipped her head to look at me. "What?"

I pointed to the cup and chuckled. "You're choking that thing."

"Ha," she replied, getting my joke now. "I get it."

I sipped from my own cup full of coffee and clenched my teeth from the sudden burst of temperature change in my mouth. My butt cheeks were growing icicles on them and then a hot substance slid down my throat, it took a minute to get used to that. Hopefully what they said was true and it would warm me from the inside out. Who knew it would get this cold here? New York, sure, but I didn't expect this from North Carolina.

Engaging in conversation with me again and seemingly getting out of her head, she asked, "How can you drink that stuff when it's so hot?"

Before I answered her, my own mind started to wander. What was she thinking about anyway? We just had a great evening at the tree lighting. Yet, she seemed perplexed almost. Honestly, it didn't bode well with me, which was probably why I tried my hand at cracking a joke. I wanted her to loosen up and smile.

Don't bother saying it, I already knew. Here, I'll go ahead and say it for you—where the heck did that come from? Well, I was changing.

Lightening up.

I supposed you could say my heart was growing two sizes too big and all that other stuff. However it went, I surely didn't know.

"Bo?" she pushed. "So how do you not burn your tongue or the roof of your mouth with it being so hot?"

I tilted my head as we continued to walk on the sidewalk, enjoying the weather (cold as it was) and this quiet night. "Isn't that sort of the whole point in ordering a hot drink? To warm you up? That only happens when it's hot."

"I like to hold it, that makes me warm enough."

"So you drink it when it's cold?"

"Not cold," she returned. "Just cooler than scorching hot."

I shrugged. "I don't get it, but then again I've always liked my food hot. I can't stand it when food sits too long and gets cold."

"Warm," she corrected.

"Tomato, tomahto."

She shook her head. "Let me explain to you where I'm coming from. I drink this hot cocoa now at this piping hot temperature and it hurts, like I-stubbed-my-toe-and-all-I-want-to-do-is-hold-it-and-rub-it hurt. Naturally, I try to soothe the pain with a cold glass of water, which makes the hot beverage a moot point because now I've got chills from the cold. Then I wake up the next morning and think it must be better, but no, the water was like a placebo, and how do I know that you ask?"

She huffed and then started up again before I had a chance to point out that I did not, in fact, ask. "Well, the skin on the roof of my mouth, the precious skin that I have come to love and adore is now hanging there flapping in the breeze."

I cleared my throat, holding back a laugh, but she widened her eyes and shot a finger out, pointing it in my direction. "Flapping," she repeated, just short of scaring me. "It's hanging on for dear life and someone call the funeral home because we need to grieve this skin that will never be the same and we all know is going to fall off. So you say goodbye to a perfectly good piece of skin that did nothing wrong and had no idea that you were going to scorch it."

All of this for a piece of skin that would grow back?

"And even after it falls off, I don't enjoy food as much, at least not for a week or so because it hurts. Oh, and don't even try eating chips because that's a real bit—"

I held up a hand and shook my head. "I'm sorry. I take back what I said. You should totally drink it at whatever temperature you want. You know your body best."

"Thank you," she said simply and took her first sip. "See, great timing, it's all about timing, Bo."

"I'm seeing that."

And now was not a good time for Izzy. She was clearly tired if she was rattling on about skin and funeral homes. . . . I honestly didn't know, so don't ask.

"Why don't I walk you home?" She wanted to show me the ice skating rink, but maybe another time would be better.

"No, come on. We have to strike while the iron is hot, and you said you wanted to see it. Who knows if you'll want to tomorrow?"

True, but the truth was, if Izzy was the one showing me, I'd want to see it anytime of day.

Then she eyed me. "Why? Did your father call and give you work or something? I thought you said you weren't dealing with anything anymore while you were here if it wasn't an emergency."

And that was still true. After we tested cake for the wedding, I realized I wanted to be more present, so I asked my father to deal with things unless I was absolutely needed. He didn't like it, but he was all right with it. Especially because he knew that I'd be back soon enough and stepping into his role.

The thing was, I didn't know if I was ready to leave.

I knew what you were thinking—you were shocked. I was, too, but it was still true.

I looked over at Izzy, who had just finished sipping more of her hot cocoa and had foam from the whipped cream on her upper lip line, like a mustache. Yeah, for the first time in a long time I felt like I was exactly where I belonged.

"It's nothing like that," I finally answered about having to get work done tonight.

"Good because I really want to show you the rink. It's beautiful and one of my favorite places to be when the weather is like this and no one is really around."

I nodded and lifted my hand, gesturing to her lip. "May I?" I asked, looking for her approval to touch her face.

She nodded, brushing a strand of her brown hair back, behind her ear. "Do I have cream on my face?"

I grinned. "You do." I wiped it with my finger and looked into her eyes, watching as she seemed to be wrestling with herself, just as I was. I leaned in closer and was shocked when her tongue darted out and she licked my finger.

She licked her lips after. "I can't waste good cream, right?"

I pushed my tongue up against the inside of my cheek. "Sure."

What an idiot I was. I couldn't believe I tried to go in for a kiss. She obviously wasn't looking for that and did that to divert the situation. Right?

I cleared my throat and went to change the subject and make things less awkward, but Izzy beat me to it, asking, "So what happened that you don't trust people?"

"Huh?" *Where did that come from?*

"Sorry, that was out of the blue." *It sure was.* "I just mean, you once asked me if I was looking to sell your story to a blog and I was wondering where that came from."

How did I tell a person like Izzy who saw the good in everyone that sometimes people were vile and self-centered? "With my position and who I am, it's hard to know who I can trust and who's just playing me."

"And you've been burned before?"

"If you mean someone used me and then hurt me with their lies, then yes."

"I'm sorry, Bo."

"Hey, what are you sorry about? You didn't do it."

"I know," she replied and peered up at me with sympathy in her eyes before grabbing my hand in hers and holding it between us. "Just so you know, I would never do that to you. I really hope you believe that."

I wasn't sure of much, but that I had no doubt about. Izzy was as loyal as they came, I had come to learn. She would do anything for the people she cared about—and she cared about a lot of people—and I counted myself lucky that I was one of those people.

"You don't know how to skate, do you?"

I shook my head. "Afraid not."

"Not tonight, but I'm going to teach you one day."

"And I'm going to fall on my butt."

"No you won't."

"What makes you say that?"

"Because I won't let you go."

* * *

It didn't take Izzy but a second to answer my question. "I'm deathly afraid of clowns." She shuddered. "I don't think there's anything quite worse than those things." Clearly feeling some sort of way (fired up from the looks of it) about the prospect of clowns, Izzy continued, "It's not one particular thing about them, either, that makes them so scary. It's just that they are creepy by their very nature." She shook her head and pointed a finger at me. "No, creepier than creepy." She angled her head. "Is there a word for that?"

I didn't know what else to do but stare at this woman who completely mesmerized me even when she was talking about clowns. I chuckled. "What is it about them that creeps you out? They're loved by children all over." I pointed out, "It's the most booked gig at birthday parties for those under the age of ten."

She swallowed. "Yeah, well, not me. I don't see how they're fun or appealing."

I swayed my head back and forth, trying to see her point. "There are multiple horror movies featuring clowns," I conceded.

"See," she practically shrieked. Then she widened her eyes. "You just proved my point."

"I gather you don't like horror movies?"

She gave me a look as though asking if I was kidding. "Of course I don't like horror movies. I prefer my cheesy, cozy romances, thank you very much." She nudged me as we walked. "What, do you like scary movies about ax murderers and, oh, I don't know, haunted houses?"

I tried stifling a laugh, but it didn't work. "Haunted houses?" I grinned.

She shrugged her shoulders. "It's the best I could come up with. I change the channel or look away when those commercials come on."

"They're not that bad," I tried convincing her. "Although, no, I don't watch them. I have seen two or three in my life, but none recently. And would I go out of my way to catch one? Nah."

She straightened her back and raised her head high, obviously pleased with my answer. "Good, because those movies aren't nice."

"Yes, and it would be wrong to watch a movie that didn't feed into the whole happily ever after bit you love so much." I didn't really care one way or the other, but watching her get all riled up, well, I enjoyed that. She was so passionate about everything. At first I wasn't sure how I felt about it, but now I was liking it.

She licked her lips and stopped walking, so I did the same and stood there, watching her looking up at me. "Is that ridiculous?" She cleared her throat. "I mean, that I believe in happily ever after. I just like to think that somewhere out there is my prince, you know?"

I cleared my own throat now, my gaze fixed on her lips. What I wouldn't give for just a taste of them. "Yeah, well, maybe you've already met him," I said and immediately regretted it. *What was I saying?* Even to my own ears it sounded like I was talking about me. "Never mind," I quickly tried to save it. "I don't think you're ridiculous, just optimistic."

I started walking again and she did, too.

"I know and you're a realist, but I think I'm okay with that. Being optimistic, I mean." She added, "I think we all could benefit from being a little bit more positive. If we are, then more good things will come our way. At least, I like to think so."

I arched a brow and peered over at her. "Something your parents told you?"

"No, actually. It's just my dad and he didn't tell me that." She giggled then. "Something I read in a book."

Regarding her closely, I stopped again and shared what was on my mind. "Don't change that, Izzy."

"Change what?" she questioned, looking confused.

"Yourself, your optimism, the way you see life." I sighed. "One day a man is going to be lucky to be able to see the world through your eyes and you'll create something beautiful together."

She smiled. "Thanks, Bo. That means a lot to me."

Pushing down my feelings that were growing much too strong for this woman, I looked away.

But she tapped my shoulder, calling my attention back to her. "And Bo?"

"Yeah?"

"I'm not changing anytime soon, so don't worry."

"Good."

* * *

In this moment, as we sat on a bench looking out at the pond that had become a quaint ice skating rink, I couldn't seem to take my eyes off Izzy. The way the moonlight was hitting her, it was like nothing I'd ever seen before. Her beauty was unmatched.

I had been through so much, but for some reason it all led me here to this moment. And it all became clear to me as I sat next to her—I didn't want to give up on the slightest possibility that Izzy and I could give this a real shot. No one knew what the future held, but I didn't care so long as I knew she would be part of that. I needed her to know that. She deserved to know, so she could figure out what she wanted, right?

I ran a hand through my hair and looked away. Geez, what was I saying? This wasn't an ideal situation. I mean, she lived here, had her whole life here, and I was in New York. I was supposed to take over my father's company. I had been groomed for that my whole life.

I had responsibilities.

But what did any of those things matter if I had no one to share them with?

And for the first time in my life I felt like there was a real chance.

Ugh, where was this coming from?

I didn't normally care about that stuff. I didn't give one iota about coming home alone, didn't want a family, traditions to pass on, holiday shenanigans.

"Bo," Izzy spoke softly, her voice sounding angelic to my ears, a total one-eighty from when I first heard her speak at the bar. She placed a hand on mine, covering it in my lap. "What's wrong?"

See, this was why I was currently thinking about what it would be like to have a household full of children, my wife and I chasing after them as they ran around rambunctiously. That was what Izzy did to me. She made me realize maybe I could have that. That I shouldn't be afraid to want that.

I looked over at her and placed my hand on her cheek, which she leaned into. Then she closed her eyes and sighed, her lips curling upward at the corners as she said, "You make me happy." Quickly, I noticed her eyes open and she swallowed hard. "I just mean. . . I didn't. . ."

I brushed my thumb over her smooth skin and offered her a smile, just like she'd always given to me. "You make me happy, too."

Her eyes looked between mine, her thumb grazing my beard just along the edge of my mouth, the curve of my lips. "What are we doing here, Bo?"

If only I knew. I chuckled and answered honestly—"For the first time, I have no idea what I'm doing, but it feels really good to not know."

She arched a brow. "You never cease to amaze me."

"That's just because I'm not open about my feelings, but I want to be open with you. I want you to know that I don't know what's going on between us, but I know I want to find out."

"Me, too," she agreed.

I leaned in slowly, my gaze going from her eyes to her lips to make sure this was really what she wanted. When she leaned in, too, I was fully prepared to kiss her and stop silencing what my heart had been trying to tell me. But then Izzy shattered the moment by blurting out, "The wedding!"

I gave her a puzzled expression, furrowing my brows and studying her now. I was trying to see if I missed a sign. I didn't think I had, so why the sudden outburst? She had to have known that would stop the kiss from happening.

She backed up and I did the same, retreating my hand from her cheek. "What about it?" I asked, even though I didn't care about the wedding right now. In fact, it was the last thing on my mind.

"I wonder how Fiona and Louie are holding up. It must be crazy knowing the next thing they know they're going to be husband and wife, married, betrothed, their wagons hitched to one another."

I cocked a brow. "I get the idea of marriage," I responded more than a little confused.

"Oh, sorry. I just can't believe it's happening so soon."

I nodded, trying to come back from the sudden one-eighty. "Yeah, me neither. We should probably get going before the sun comes up." It was pretty late and like she said, the wedding was no small thing and we had to be ready for the ceremony tomorrow.

"You're right," she said, snapping her fingers and getting up.

I followed suit and we began walking back. "Thanks for taking me here."

"Thanks for being such great company," she replied with her usual smile, like nothing was just about to happen.

Maybe it was for the best.

Chapter Fifteen

Izzy

What was it about weddings that made you think about your own love life? Or lack thereof, in my case.

Oh, and please don't remind me about the whole ice skating rink debacle. Yes, that was what we were calling it. You could also call it the moment that Izzy's brain fell out of her head and she decided to do the stupidest thing ever and cut the moment short, but I preferred the debacle one because it was shorter. To each their own, though.

And it didn't matter what you chose to call it because I couldn't seem to get the moment out of my head. And why not? Well, besides the fact that I'd be winning the award for this year's biggest idiot, I was currently sitting at the same table as Bo, watching our best friends dance their first dance.

The ceremony was beautiful and everything I'd imagined it would be. This wasn't the first wedding I'd attended, but it was the first I helped plan and I didn't think I'd ever stop obsessing over how romantic and inspiring it all was.

This was the moment, the day that little girls (me included) dreamed about. I wanted to walk down the aisle in a white poofy dress that I got lost in, naturally, to marry the love of my life, the one person in the whole world who understood me and saw me for me.

I thought I knew what I wanted, what I was looking for, but it turned out you couldn't set expectations on love, Zel was right about that. You couldn't plan for who your soulmate would be or what they'd be like. It just sort of had to happen. It was like a fairytale—only, because I was sabotaging myself, mine wouldn't end with a kiss. Mine wouldn't happen at all. Need I remind you that Bo was only here for a short period of time, that he was leaving to head back to New York soon?

And that was why I didn't see the point in kissing him at the rink. I didn't want my heart to hurt any more than it would when I had to say goodbye.

Long distance relationships didn't work.

I knew this.

I'd been down this road before.

And I knew people said that with the right person everything would fall into place, but wasn't that merely wishful thinking?

I was all for optimism, but not if it meant breaking my own heart. I didn't want to feel like a piece of me was missing every time we were apart. This was for the best, for both of us, but especially me.

Pushing thoughts of my own love life aside, I couldn't help the smile that took over as I observed Fiona laughing as Louie spun her, her head falling back. I didn't think I had ever seen her this happy. Being with Louie always put a smile on her face, but today was something else entirely. It appeared being his wife suited her.

When the emcee announced it was time for other couples to join the happy couple on the dance floor, I shifted in my seat and tapped on Bo's shoulder, trying to get his attention.

Bo always looked handsome, but tonight, in his best man attire, he looked dashing as ever, wearing a navy blue suit and grey tie. Plus, it complimented my yellow maid of honor dress nicely. To the outside world, we looked like the perfect couple.

And I really believed we could be—at least our definition of perfect.

So why was I pushing him away when all I wanted to do was hold him close?

"Want to dance?" I asked, placing a hand out for him to take as I got up, hoping he wouldn't leave me hanging.

Peering up at me now, he looked from me to my hand, but shook his head. "I don't think so."

"Come on, please? Don't make me pull someone else out onto the dance floor." I didn't want to feel someone else's hands on me. I wanted to be held by him—why couldn't he see that?

He looked around and cleared his throat. "I'm sure any man here would be more than willing to dance with you."

Why was he being like this? I stood my ground. "I want to dance with you." I emphasized that last word.

He straightened his shoulders and told me, "I don't dance."

"You don't or you won't?"

"Both."

I rolled my eyes. "Well, that's not good enough." I pleaded, "Please, Bo. We look snow cute. We wouldn't want to waste it sitting in these chairs off to the side when there's a lovely ballroom floor we could be dancing on."

He snorted. "Snow cute?" he repeated.

Of course that was what he caught on to.

"Fine." He placed his hand in mine and led the way to the dance floor. "But only one dance and then I'm coming to sit back down and wait for the cake to come out."

"You're looking forward to that cake, are you?"

He narrowed his eyes. "It's chocolate cake, of course I'm looking forward to it."

I chuckled as we stepped into each other's embrace, my arms wrapping around his neck as we moved to the soft music. "Is it Louie that likes chocolate or you?"

Grinning, he replied, "Can't it be both?"

"May I ask you something?"

He stepped back, extending his arms, his hands still around my waist, but now our eyes could meet. "Anything," he answered and I knew he meant it.

I waited to get up the courage to ask what was on my mind. When it finally came, I came out with it—"If I asked you to come back, would you?"

He furrowed his brows. "You mean in the new year?"

I nodded. "I'd really like it if you did."

"What for?"

He couldn't be serious. He didn't know? I wet my lips, intending on being as obvious as possible without outright saying it. "For me." Then I tried again, but this time was more specific. "For us."

Brows furrowed, he asked, "Us?"

"Bo, don't make me spell it out." Not that I was sure I knew why I'd have to. I mean, did I really have to? Maybe there wasn't an us yet, but there could have been. Wasn't he there for that almost-kiss last night? I knew he wanted it as much as I did. Could he have gotten over whatever this was already?

He grew rigid and seemingly less comfortable, his expression looking more serious, too. "Maybe I need you to."

Fine, if he needed me to say it, then I would. "I want to be with you. I want you to stay so that we can date each other." Okay, that sounded lame. It sounded a lot more romantic in my head.

He looked perplexed, like he wanted to say yes, but he was holding back, stopping himself. "I don't think that's such a good idea," he finally said, looking as crestfallen as I felt.

"Why not? You were about to kiss me at the rink. I know you feel something here. Don't you want to give us a chance to see what this could be? We could have the greatest fairytale ever told."

"This isn't one of your books, Izzy," he said and when the song ended, without hesitation, Bo walked out of my embrace and started toward the door.

I knew what you were thinking. I shouldn't want to be with a man who wasn't going to fight for me, who was going to leave me alone on a dance floor, or walk away when things got hard. But I couldn't help it, I wanted him. I wanted Bo.

Because I knew that he wasn't the man he saw himself to be or the way others saw him, either. He was more than that.

Sure, he could be beastly, but if that was the case and we were going to call him a beast, then I wanted him to be *my* beast.

Then again, we didn't always get what we wanted, did we?

I was just afraid this would be one of those times.

* * *

Bo

I had to get out of there.

It was starting to feel like the walls were closing in on me and it was getting harder for me to breathe the longer I stayed.

It didn't matter how far I was from the venue because Izzy's words were still ringing in my ear, "Don't you want to give us a chance?"

Of course I wanted to give us a chance! I wanted to know if there even was an us. Man, I really wished there was.

But how could there be an us, dummy, if you keep walking away from the possibility?

Yes, the first time it was Izzy that stopped things from progressing, but I didn't help matters. I ended things just as fast, agreeing we should get some sleep. And the entire walk back to her place, it was crickets. Frigging crickets. I didn't so much as hear her shiver from the chill in the air.

The only thing that was left to feed my soul was the annoyance I felt for being so stupid.

But I had to let her go because how could she ever be happy with a man like me? Izzy was a heck of a woman and she could have any man she wanted. It wasn't like we'd get some happily ever after.

This was real life. Not some romance book. She was wrong, there would be no fairytale ending.

And the sooner I got out of this town, the sooner I could forget about all of this and move on with my life.

Give me some time and I was sure I could get past Izzy and everything I liked about her. Her adorable behavior. *Adorable behavior?* Why did that pop into my head?

But it was cute how she acted sometimes, wasn't it? Like the way she was so passionate about the silliest of things.

Candy canes.

Tree decorating.

Wedding cake.

Christmas.

Christmas.

Did I mention Christmas?

Even when she was practically dragging me into Jesse's house for an ugly sweater party, I couldn't deny how cute she was, trying to get me to feel better about my sweater by pointing out an even uglier one.

She also had one of the biggest hearts I'd ever seen. I wasn't the easiest person to get along with when we first met or when we started planning our friends' wedding over email. None of that deterred her, though. She put our differences aside and tried to find the good in me, in all of it.

In the meantime, I fell for her—hard. But I couldn't forget this wasn't some fantasy.

As I walked across the street and onto the sidewalk, I played every memory we shared in my head like it was a movie reel. To be honest, it could easily be one of my favorite movies. Only, I didn't think I liked the ending of this one.

"Bo!" I heard someone shout to me. It wasn't someone, though. I would know that voice anywhere. It was Izzy.

I turned around and watched as she continued walking, crossing the street to come straight to me. She was wearing a long, white and gray coat over her dress now and she looked even more radiant enveloped in the fur. I drank her in and couldn't help the smile that tugged at my lips. This woman was incredible.

But what was she holding? My eyes honed in on the small box in her hands and I cocked a brow, curious what was inside.

Before I could think any further about the box or anything else for that matter, I heard an engine and the sound was getting closer until finally I looked to our side and saw a motorcycle coming down the street. . . and fast. It wasn't stopping, so my eyes went from the motorcycle to

Izzy, who was walking in the middle of the street coming straight toward me, but not fast enough.

I ran in the street without even thinking twice about it and pushed Izzy out of harm's way, bringing us both down to the ground that was cushioned with soft white snow from this morning's snowfall. The motorcycle drove right past us, not a care in the world.

"Who was that?" I asked aloud, but knew she couldn't tell me since she looked as surprised by all of that as I was.

She shook her head, her mouth agape. "I have no idea, but it was definitely no one from around here."

"How could you be so sure? Because there's sixteen hundred people who live here?" I asked, knowing I'd get a rise out of her with that one.

"Sixteen hundred and two," she returned as I expected, laughing. Then she explained, "No one from around here would be driving so recklessly on Christmas Eve."

I got up and lended her my hand to help her up, too. "Are you okay?"

She dusted herself off with the hand that wasn't holding the box still firmly in her grasp, and nodded. "I think so. Thanks to you."

"Don't make me out to be some prince."

"Sorry." She shrugged. "You earned the title."

Ignoring her comment, not wanting to give her any other reason to believe I was this great guy, I only said, "Maybe we should get out of the street."

As we stepped back on the sidewalk, I questioned, "Why are you here, anyway?"

"You mean, why did I come after you?"

I cracked my knuckles nervously, waiting, hoping she wouldn't say what I thought she was about to say, and looked her in the eyes expectantly.

She exhaled. "I'm not going to let you walk away."

And she said it, folks.

"Excuse me?"

"This isn't only about you. I'm involved, too. And I deserve a say, don't I?" But before I could respond, she went on, saying, "Every year Silver Springs celebrates Christmas with the tradition of hanging our coveted personalized ornaments on the tree in the center of town. We gather and hang our ball and those of loved ones that have come before us or are no longer here to hang it themselves for whatever reason."

Why was she telling me this? "I know this. I was there."

She shook her head. "Maybe so, but this next part you don't know."

I tilted my head and quirked a brow. What didn't I know? It seemed pretty basic to me. It was for the townspeople, a tradition they had to get them all together and celebrate the holidays. What was I missing?

Pushing the box she was holding now toward me, she urged, "Take it. It's for you. An early Christmas present."

I couldn't accept this. Especially not when I didn't get her anything. "You shouldn't have," I spoke my mind.

She brushed me off, though, and insisted I see what was inside. "I won't take no for an answer and didn't your parents ever teach you it's not nice to turn down a gift?"

I sighed and took the box. "I'll open it later." Say when I was halfway back to New York, where I belonged. I didn't belong here with Izzy. I had never done anything to deserve her. She was too good. Too. . . sunshiney. *Was that a word?* Well, either way, it was the best way to describe her and I was sticking with it.

She put a hand on her hip now and gave me a look that all but said *I don't think so* as she dared me to change my mind.

"What do you want from me?" I didn't know how many more times I could walk away from her. Without telling her how I felt.

"What do I want?" she echoed my words. "I want you to open that box and see that it's all I could do not to think about you. You've gotten under my skin, Beauregard."

I swallowed at the use of my full name, remembering one of the first times she cracked the armor I had around my heart. Izzy definitely wrecked my plans of never letting someone in enough to hurt me again. But I was okay with that if it meant I could be with her.

I didn't know what I was waiting for exactly. Maybe a sledgehammer to hit me over the head and remind me why this was a bad idea.

Without hesitating anymore, I opened the box to reveal a Christmas ball, but not just any Christmas ball. This one was just for me. It was white with blue snowflakes and my name in block letters: Bo.

I must've been holding my breath because when Izzy's eyes filled with water and her voice cracked as she asked, "Do you like it?" I found it hard to find my own voice.

So I decided not to overthink it and placed it back in the box and put it in one hand so that I could easily lift her up and twirl her around.

She giggled as I spun us and the only thing I could think as she smiled down at me was that this was all I wanted, all I needed: for her to be happy. Just like this.

"So I take it you like it?" she joked as I put her down, her feet touching the ground again.

I nodded. "You could say that."

With our faces mere inches from one another, I brought a finger to her bottom lip and pulled on it slightly until she opened her mouth, her breath hitting my hand as she said, "Please tell me you're going to kiss me."

I smiled. "Yeah, I'm going to kiss you," I promised before bringing my lips down on hers.

The kiss started out slow, like we were getting to know one another all over again, and didn't want to take things too fast. But once she opened her mouth to me, I couldn't help but quicken the pace, sliding my tongue in and relishing in her sweet taste. If I didn't know any better I'd think she ate a candy cane before coming here because she tasted sweet and minty.

The kiss was never-ending and you'd hear no complaints from me about that, but finally I leaned my forehead against hers as we both tried to catch our breath.

"Best kiss ever," she whispered, sighing happily.

I gave her another quick kiss on the lips and agreed with her.

She laughed. Then she asked, "So what now?"

I grabbed her hand in mine and squeezed it tight. "Now we go on a proper date."

She blushed, her cheeks turning that crimson color I loved. "Oh, Bo, are you asking me out on a date?"

"I am," I answered, smiling. "I'll even pull out your chair for you."

"Will this date end in another kiss?"

I let out a low growl. "If I have it my way, it'll start with one, too."

"Good. So we're on the same page."

"Seems so."

"Who knew," she began asking, her cheerfulness filling the cold air, "that two people like us, as different as day and night, would end up together?"

"I wasn't so sure we would for a second, but I guess even a beast like me could find love with a beauty like you."

Epilogue

Bo

THE FUTURE

I **walked hand in** hand with Izzy, looking around at the now familiar town that I would call home, at least for a few months out of the year.

Izzy teased me when I made the decision, saying that now the town had sixteen-hundred and three residents. If I was being honest, the moment we decided to be together and give this a shot, the number no longer mattered to me, especially if she wanted to officially count me in. Sure, it was small and everyone seemed to know everyone (and their business), but I wanted to be wherever Izzy was.

And every time it came time for me to leave Silver Springs and head back to New York, it felt like a piece of me was missing. That was because I was leaving her behind. That was why we decided to make some changes.

We had been together for a while now and it was obvious Izzy and I had something special, so on my last visit to town we talked about my working from here when I could. One of the perks of being CEO, you could say. No longer under my father's thumb, I was able to finally make decisions for the company that I saw fit. You had no idea what that did for a man, especially when you had the parents I did.

Well, that and Izzy—okay, so maybe there were two things that changed my life recently. That was the whole reason why I wasn't ready to let her go, not yet. Dare I say, not ever.

Which brought us here. . . I pulled open the door to the new tattoo parlor in town.

Do you remember that motorcycle that breezed through town without a care in the world and almost ran Izzy over? Yeah, well, that motorcycle was owned by Flynn Cavallo, as was this tattoo parlor. And yes, I was over the fact that he could've hurt Izzy. It wasn't good to harp on things, especially things we couldn't change—at least that was how Izzy told it to me.

Anyway, this place didn't get the warmest of welcomes at first, but I liked it. It brought a new angle to the small town, something interesting. Now, as for Flynn—*yes, we all know you're curious about him*—well, his is a story you'll have to wait for because he had been keeping to himself and no one knew much about him or what brought him to town, so I couldn't exactly say.

I looked around and studied all the sketches on the walls, sketches of tattoo designs. I wondered if Flynn had drawn these himself. Some tattoo artists were known to sketch their own designs, but others didn't. And these sketches were certainly unique. I'll give you an idea of what I was talking about:

A horse with a sword in his mouth as though getting ready to charge toward someone or something.

The back of a woman with long blonde hair that seemed to be glowing.

A green chameleon with its tongue sticking out.

A frying pan with a sun emblazoned on it. This one almost looked mystical. Except why a frying pan, I wondered. *What was with that?*

I looked over at Izzy, who was staring at the curtain hanging on a doorway separating the front from the back. She stiffened beside me and her eyes grew wide. "You know what, we can just go home. Yeah, let's go."

I squeezed her hand. "It's going to be okay."

I knew she was worried about my decision to get a tattoo. She said that it was too permanent a decision and that I needed more time to think on it. But I had considered it many times before and always thought getting one would be cool. It wasn't getting a tattoo that was the problem, it was what I should get it of. What did I want marked on my skin forever?

Then I met Izzy and I knew the answer to that one.

And no, it was not of her face. That would be creepy. Sorry to anyone who had a tattoo of their partner's face, but that wasn't something I'd be doing.

Plus, I was pretty sure Izzy wouldn't find it endearing.

"You're sure about this?" she questioned.

I nodded slowly, completely sure about this and my decision. At one time I might've given a sarcastic or quipped response, but now I spoke from my heart. "As sure as I am about you."

Just then, Flynn walked out from the back, raking a hand through his brown hair. "Hey, what can I do for you?" he asked, looking from me to Izzy.

Walking over, I went to shake his hand. "I'm Bo and this is my girlfriend, Izzy."

I didn't need to look at Izzy to know she was blushing, her cheeks turning that shade of red I'd seen dozens of times before. It happened every time I called her my girlfriend and I didn't hate it, either, when she used the label boyfriend for me.

"I'd like a tattoo," I said, stating the obvious.

He laughed and slapped his hands together. "You don't say? You know, you're the first, and I got to say, I'm pretty glad to see someone walk in here," he remarked. At least him being glad didn't mean he was smiling like the Cheshire cat. No, that was more my M.O. these days. Give the dude some time here, though, and knowing this town, he'd be humming happy tunes as he walked down the street to get to the grocery store soon enough.

It was nice to see a face like mine, er, my old one—straight-lipped and serious.

I offered him a smile. "Yeah, well, I always wanted one, so I figured why wait any longer. Let's do this."

Flynn nodded. "Sounds good to me. Come on back. Will you be coming, too?" he asked of Izzy, who now had her attention on a sketchbook on the counter.

Looking at her, too, now, I shook my head to Flynn and laid a hand on the small of her back, whispering in her ear, "I'd like to surprise you, if you don't mind."

She looked up, her attention back on me and the look of fear returning to her eyes. "Okay, but I'm still nervous."

You don't say, I thought to myself.

Her eyes looked deep into mine, as though searching for an answer. "What are you getting again?" she asked, her eyebrows raised as she waited for me to tell her.

There we go, that was the million-dollar question, wasn't it?

But we both knew I wasn't saying. She had asked me a dozen times before and I didn't tell her then, so there was no chance I was telling her now. I stuck to what I said before.

"Something special. Something to signify the way you changed my life."

Grimacing, she bit her bottom lip. "All right. Be like that."

I walked over and kissed her on the cheek. "It'll be fine and you'll love it."

"It's going to hurt," she warned for the umpteenth time since I brought the idea up. Then she turned to Flynn and looked for confirmation on that one. "Right?"

He laughed. "It'll barely tickle," he answered her and walked to the curtain, holding it back. "You ready?"

I nodded and rubbed her shoulder before turning to join him in the back. "Relax. I'll be out before you know it. Then we can go home and—"

Her eyes grew wide and looked over to where Flynn was standing, waiting.

"Order takeout," I finished and her eyes went back to their normal size.

"I can't wait," she replied. She clutched her purse to her chest and nodded, a smile finally crossing her lips. That was a smile I needed to see, one that I now craved. It was funny how things changed, wasn't it?

I returned her smile before walking through the curtain with Flynn.

* * *

"You know, that was better than usual and I especially liked the sticky rice," Izzy noted of our dinner.

We were sitting on the couch, her feet curled up on the couch as she leaned into me, her head on my shoulder and my arm draped over hers.

The number of times she'd asked me if she could see it or if I could just "put her out of her misery" and tell her: eight.

Although, I had a feeling we were inching close to nine at this point.

I had a timer on my phone that would ding when it was safe to take the bandage off. Good thing I didn't get a larger tattoo because that would've made the wait time even longer and I didn't think Izzy could handle that.

I checked my phone that was on the arm of the couch and saw we had three minutes left. That wasn't so bad, right?

"The sticky rice was good," I agreed, trying to appease her with small talk.

She threw her head back now and groaned. "Bo, this is torture. If you just tell me, then I won't give a hoot when that thing comes off. But you're killing me here."

"Patience is a virtue."

"Yes," she said, "but that's not a virtue I possess." Then she pointed a finger in my face. "And you know that about me."

I took her finger and kissed it before pulling her close and kissing the top of her forehead. "Yes, I do know that."

"So you accept that about me because you have to," she told me. "Just as I accept that you're putting me through this when you could easily tell me. He who has the knowledge and all of that," she said, her words trailing off.

What? I cocked a brow.

She rolled her eyes. "You know what I mean." She blurted out, "I can't believe you won't tell me, show me, whatever."

"One more minute," I informed her after looking at my phone again. "When you hear my phone go off, you can do the honors and take the bandage off."

"Really?" Her whole face practically lit up. "I'll be really gentle. I've been watching videos, actually."

"I know."

"You know?" She arched a brow. "How do you know?"

I shrugged. "I've walked in the room and seen you staring at your screen watching videos."

Looking unashamed, she turned to face me. "Well, I just wanted to make sure I knew everything there was to know about tattoos and caring for them, so that I could take care of you."

No one had ever wanted to take care of me before. For so long I could only depend on myself, so it was nice to know that I had found that with Izzy.

At the noise coming from my phone, we were finally alerted to the fact that it was time for me to take off the bandage. Although, if the timer didn't alert me, then Izzy would've because she was already standing up, bouncing on the balls of her feet. Her excitement level practically through the roof, which had to have been contagious because I said, "Okay, okay. You can take it off," as I smiled at her.

She sat back down next to me and carefully rolled up the sleeve of my shirt and studied the bandage. "If you want, you can do it."

I grabbed her hand that was in her lap, bringing it to my lips. "No. You got this. I trust you implicitly."

Her face aglow at my words, I chuckled. "What? Like you didn't know that to be true already?"

She leaned over and brushed a kiss on my lips. I pulled her in by the back of her neck and tried to deepen it, but she pulled back. "No way! There's no time for that right now." She wagged a finger at me. "I want to see this tattoo."

"And to think," I began, feigning disappointment, "I thought kissing me would get your mind off of it. I thought I was a world-class kisser."

She blushed. "You've got skills, I'll give you that." Then she added, "And we're definitely going to go back to that, but right now I really want to see your tattoo."

"I'm counting on it."

With a hand near the bandage, she looked up at me momentarily before focusing her attention back on the bandage. She rubbed the skin around the bandage before finding a corner and lifting it off. In the slowest reveal ever, she finally sat back, bandage in hand, and gasped softly.

My gut clenched at the sound I knew so well, the sound she made when she was truly surprised, but also truly happy.

Her eyes began to water and in that moment I knew I made the right decision, not just about the bandage, but about her. I didn't think I could imagine the cookie crumbling any other way for me. I was meant to come to this town and plan a wedding—our friends' wedding—with this woman.

And to think, I thought no one could care for a beast like me.

But she did.

She did, and it quite literally saved me.

Her voice was barely above a whisper as she croaked, "It's a rose."

"For you," I pointed out, knowing I really didn't need to, but wasn't sure what else to say.

"It's beautiful, Bo." Then she took my face in her hands and leaned in to give me a kiss on the lips.

It was a short kiss again and I would've preferred that we stayed like that for a while longer, but she pulled back and smiled, looking at the opened red rose that now adorned my arm. "It's a rose for me," she repeated as though letting it fully absorb in.

I grazed my thumb over her cheek to wipe away a tear that had fallen. "What did you expect me to get?"

She looked at me. I mean, really looked at me, her eyes going from one to the other and then back again. "I have no idea." She exhaled, clearly trying to avoid having more tears fall. "Not this. This is the sweetest thing anyone has ever done for me."

I wrapped my arms around her, bringing her close.

She rested her head on my shoulder.

"It's a tale as old as time," I explained. "Beast meets girl and girl shows him what it's like to truly be loved." I kissed her hair and, not for the first time, really appreciated how far we came and all that she did for me, for my life.

"It's an enchanting story," she said, amusement in her voice.

That it was, but, in fact, it was better because it was real. This story was ours. "As enchanting as you, as enchanting as my rose."

For Izzy Rose Monroe changed my life and I, Bo Grant, was no longer the beast I saw myself to be, but a prince among men for having landed a woman as special as her.

Thank You

I hope you enjoyed reading I hope you enjoyed reading Bo and Izzy's grumpy x sunshine rom-com!

If you did, please consider leaving a review. Reviews are so important and I appreciate your time and support.

SILVER SPRINGS #2

If you loved Silver Springs and can't wait to go back, then don't worry because something tells me we'll be right back here the same time next year. Zel is getting her own story in *It's Not All Reindeer Games* and I can't wait for you to get to know her man (hint, hint: he owns a certain tattoo parlor and is new in town). Flynn makes her feel like the world has shifted on its axis and it's only because of each other that they finally see the light.

Don't Tell Me Twice Sneak Peek

Perla

LITTLE LESS THAN A YEAR AGO

I LOOKED PATHETIC.

Look at the poor, lonely girl sitting all by herself at a table for two in a nice restaurant in New York. That was what everyone was probably thinking as they passed by me.

And why wouldn't they be thinking that?

To some extent, it was true. I was sitting here like I didn't have a friend in the world, stuck in dinner purgatory, refusing to order without him but not ready to move on either and get up to leave.

You see, I had dinner plans with my boyfriend, Chris. He asked me out tonight, he made the reservations, and he told me to show up and that he'd meet me here. Naturally, I did because, silly me, I believed him. Again.

Now before you jump to the conclusion that I was a pushover, some lovesick puppy that clearly couldn't see her boyfriend was standing her up, let me explain. Chris and I had been together for a while. He was a great guy, but he was busy. He was working hard at his job and trying to prove himself to anyone worth caring.

And here I was making excuses for him. Because that was what it certainly sounded like to my own ears.

My eyes darted over my shoulder at the happy couple in the corner of the room, his hand holding hers from across the table, the smiles on their faces as radiant as could be expected from a couple in love.

Was I smiling, though? No. No, I was not.

So why did I stay with him?

Well, I couldn't exactly say. I supposed there were a lot of reasons I stayed with him, one of the more prominent ones being: I loved Christopher.

But could you ever really love a man who was rarely around?

* * *

Frankie

"Frankie, I'm glad I got you," Christopher announced as soon as I picked up his call.

I locked my front door and turned to walk to my car in the driveway, checking my watch. He'd better make this quick, I thought, I had a date to get to. "Oh, yeah, why's that?"

"I'm supposed to meet Perla for dinner. She's already there, waiting for me."

I looked up and silently wished that these words weren't coming out of his mouth. This was becoming a bit of a pattern with Chris and I wasn't sure why it was my problem. Sure, he was my best friend, but lately he was being a real jerk and I didn't feel like cleaning up his messes anymore. "Doesn't your girlfriend have a driver?" Her family was loaded, like Long Island royalty, she certainly didn't need me to chauffeur her around when her father had one on his payroll.

"I already called him, he's in the city picking up Angelo from a business trip." I better explain: Angelo was Perla's father.

I opened the door to my Mercedes and slid in. "You know, I have a date of my own. I'm on my way to meet her now." It wasn't like I was a lonely sap just sitting around on a Saturday night.

"Please," Chris pleaded. "I'll owe you one."

I shook my head. If we counted every single time I'd done this for him, then he definitely owed me a lot more than one, but I wasn't about to go there. "You know, you're lucky we've been friends since high school because for anyone else," I reminded him, letting my words fall off.

Brushing me off, he said, "Yeah, I know."

"Ten years, dude, but whatever's been going on with you lately is bad. You need to get your act together. I'm sure your girl doesn't like it, either."

"She understands."

Why did I doubt that? "Text me the restaurant. I'll pick her up." Already texting to cancel my date, I hung up, not willing to listen to him for another second. It was all lies, it always was, but it was Chris.

Did you ever have that one friend, the one who really was a lousy friend, but you would never turn your back on anyway? At least not until they did something heinous? That was Chris.

He didn't try to be a bad guy, but he just couldn't seem to be any other way. And it wasn't just me, our entire friend group saw it. We had no idea what was going on with Chris lately, but it'd been getting worse, especially where his girlfriend was concerned. I knew work was kicking his butt lately, but he'd passed her off on us so many times, I wasn't sure if he was looking for her to break up with him or what. Not that Perla would do that, she was much too kind and sweet to not listen to his excuses, to not accept them. Not that she was a pushover, but she had this nice quality to her. But nice didn't change the fact that she was Chris's girl and I much preferred spending my time with girls I was into. Although, I'd been pushed into scenarios like the one right now, where I'd have to spend time with her, and it was never a bad time. Just awkward.

As I pulled up to the restaurant, a five-star place in Smithtown, I parked and walked in, slipping on my suit jacket as I went, ready to either deliver the news that Chris wouldn't be coming or act like I understood what was going on here. I never knew which one it'd be. Sometimes he told her, other times he left it for me to deliver the news.

I spotted her at a table in the back by the fireplace and pointed. "I'm here to meet a friend," I told the maître d', who nodded and let me back.

She was holding the menu, looking at it casually, sipping her water.

As I walked up, I decided I knew which way it was going to go—I had to tell her Chris wasn't coming.

Surprising her, I walked right up and tapped her on the shoulder. "Perla," I started, my stomach sick over doing this, again.

As signs of confusion left her face, she put the menu down. "He's not coming, is he?" She pushed her chair back without a word from me. "I actually thought he'd make it tonight. He'd been promising to take me here for weeks."

As I watched her, she went from confused to sad, disappointed almost. It would never not kill me to do this. *What was Chris thinking?* "Wait," I said stopping her. "We're both here. I had to cancel a date anyway, so I say we stay."

"What? You cancelled a date to pick me up?" she asked, a hand on her chest.

At ease with my decision, I answered, "It's no big deal, but what do you say we stay and eat something? I'm hungry, so you'd be doing me a favor."

She looked around as if unsure.

"Please," I added.

Finally, she nodded. "Okay, but we use Chris's credit card. He had to leave it on file when he booked our reservation."

I smiled, surprised by how resilient she was, how wily. "You got it. I think I saw a nice-looking steak in some guy's dish on the way over, maybe I'll get that." I pulled out the chair opposite of her and sat down.

"Wagyu," she noted of the steak. "Let's make it two." She laughed and picked up her menu again, perusing it with grace. "Thanks, Frankie," she expressed from behind her menu.

"It's nothing." It was obvious what Chris saw in her, but I had no idea what she saw in him. What any of us did..

Want more from Perla and Frankie's story? This ex's best friend, marriage of convenience rom-com *Don't Tell Me Twice* is the first book in The Morelli Sisters interconnected standalone series.

Also by Dani Ryan

THE RYDER BROTHERS

A series of interconnected standalone contemporary romances

Forever My Protector

Forever My Ranger

Forever My Soldier

Forever My Guardian

THE HURRICANES

A series of interconnected standalone rom-coms

It Just Happened

THE MORELLI SISTERS

A series of interconnected standalone rom-coms

Don't Tell Me Twice

Say It Isn't So

About the Author

Dani Ryan is an author of romantic comedies and contemporary romances that have spice without the spice. She's also a momma to a diva doggie, although she wouldn't have it any other way. She loves coffee, carrots with hummus is her favorite snack, and sometimes she likes to indulge in a margarita (preferably during the summer when she's on the water).

Follow Dani Ryan on social for new release updates, book deals, and exclusive content, she's @daniryanbooks everywhere.

Subscribe to her newsletter for all the latest and a bonus scene from one of her books.

And, of course, don't forget to check out Dani Ryan's reader's group on Facebook where you can swoon for days! Just search Dani Ryan's Swooners.

Milton Keynes UK
Ingram Content Group UK Ltd.
UKHW040940141024
449705UK00005B/202

9 798330 397976